MW01410443

PEOPLE IN THE NEWS

Nicolas Cage

by Corinne J. Naden and Rose Blue

LUCENT BOOKS®

THOMSON ™
★
GALE

San Diego • Detroit • New York • San Francisco • Cleveland
New Haven, Conn. • Waterville, Maine • London • Munich

THOMSON

GALE

On cover: Actor Nicolas Cage is pictured in a movie still for the film *Windtalkers*.

© 2003 by Lucent Books. Lucent Books is an imprint of The Gale Group, Inc., a division of Thomson Learning, Inc.

Lucent Books® and Thomson Learning™ are trademarks used herein under license.

For more information, contact
Lucent Books
27500 Drake Rd.
Farmington Hills, MI 48331-3535
Or you can visit our Internet site at http://www.gale.com

ALL RIGHTS RESERVED.
No part of this work covered by the copyright hereon may be reproduced or used in any form or by any means—graphic, electronic, or mechanical, including photocopying, recording, taping, Web distribution or information storage retrieval systems—without the written permission of the publisher.

LIBRARY OF CONGRESS CATALOGING-IN-PUBLICATION DATA

Naden, Corinne J.
   Nicolas Cage / by Corinne J. Naden and Rose Blue
   p. cm. — (People in the news)
Summary: Presents the life and career of the movie actor who was born Nicolas Kim Coppola.
Includes bibliographical references and index.
   ISBN 1-59018-136-0 (hardback : alk. paper)
   1. Cage, Nicolas, 1965- —Juvenile literature. 2. Motion picture actors and actresses—United States—Biography—Juvenile literature. [1. Cage, Nicolas, 1965- 2. Actors and actresses.] I. Blue, Rose. II. Title. III. People in the News (San Diego, Calif.)
   PN2287.C227 N33 2003
   791.43'028'092—dc21
 	
   2002151097

Printed in the United States of America

Table of Contents

Foreword	4
Introduction	
Instead of Jail	6
Chapter 1	
Destined for the Screen	8
Chapter 2	
Odd Man Out	25
Chapter 3	
Toward a New Image	40
Chapter 4	
All Roads Leave from Vegas	56
Chapter 5	
The Professional Nonconformist	69
Notes	79
Important Dates in the Life of Nicolas Cage	83
For Further Reading	85
Works Consulted	87
Index	91
Picture Credits	95
About the Authors	96

Foreword

FAME AND CELEBRITY are alluring. People are drawn to those who walk in fame's spotlight, whether they are known for great accomplishments or for notorious deeds. The lives of the famous pique public interest and attract attention, perhaps because their experiences seem in some ways so different from, yet in other ways so similar to, our own.

Newspapers, magazines, and television regularly capitalize on this fascination with celebrity by running profiles of famous people. For example, television programs such as *Entertainment Tonight* devote all of their programming to stories about entertainment and entertainers. Magazines such as *People* fill their pages with stories of the private lives of famous people. Even newspapers, newsmagazines, and television news frequently delve into the lives of well-known personalities. Despite the number of articles and programs, few provide more than a superficial glimpse at their subjects.

Lucent's People in the News series offers young readers a deeper look into the lives of today's newsmakers, the influences that have shaped them, and the impact they have had in their fields of endeavor and on other people's lives. The subjects of the series hail from many disciplines and walks of life. They include authors, musicians, athletes, political leaders, entertainers, entrepreneurs, and others who have made a mark on modern life and who, in many cases, will continue to do so for years to come.

These biographies are more than factual chronicles. Each book emphasizes the contributions, accomplishments, or deeds that have brought fame or notoriety to the individual and shows how that person has influenced modern life. Authors portray their subjects in a realistic, unsentimental light. For example, Bill Gates—the cofounder and chief executive officer of the software giant Microsoft—has been instrumental in making personal computers the most vital tool of the modern age. Few dispute his business savvy, his perseverance, or his technical expertise, yet critics say he is ruthless in his dealings with competitors and driven more by his desire to maintain Microsoft's dominance in the computer industry than by an interest in furthering technology.

In these books, young readers will encounter inspiring stories about real people who achieved success despite enormous obstacles. Oprah Winfrey—the most powerful, most watched, and wealthiest woman on television today—spent the first six years of her life in the care of her grandparents while her unwed mother sought work and a better life elsewhere. Her adolescence was colored by promiscuity, pregnancy at age fourteen, rape, and sexual abuse.

Each author documents and supports his or her work with an array of primary and secondary source quotations taken from diaries, letters, speeches, and interviews. All quotes are footnoted to show readers exactly how and where biographers derive their information and provide guidance for further research. The quotations enliven the text by giving readers eyewitness views of the life and accomplishments of each person covered in the People in the News series.

In addition, each book in the series includes photographs, annotated bibliographies, timelines, and comprehensive indexes. For both the casual reader and the student researcher, the People in the News series offers insight into the lives of today's newsmakers—people who shape the way we live, work, and play in the modern age.

Introduction

Instead of Jail

Long known as a genuine talent with a flair for the unconventional, Nicolas Cage has become one of Hollywood's biggest stars. He has been called offbeat, weird, and even bizarre, both in his choice of films and his offscreen life. Yet Cage ignores his critics and follows his own path, a path that has brought him professional praise and one Academy Award for his portrayal of a hopeless alcoholic in *Leaving Las Vegas* (1995).

Cage not only likes his work in Hollywood, but he thinks that Hollywood saved his life. At least, that is the impression he gives when he says, "I had a temper—I could do things very spontaneously. If it wasn't for acting I probably wouldn't have been able to channel it. I would probably be in jail."[1] Instead, Cage is in the movie business with more than forty-five films to his credit.

Nicolas Cage fits in naturally with the movie industry because much of his family has been involved in it, most notably his director uncle Francis Ford Coppola (*The Godfather* movies) and his actress aunt Talia Shire (*The Godfather, Part 2*). Cage, however, was determined to make a reputation for himself.

Cage did succeed on his own, but his film choices—especially in the first several years of his career—were called by most film critics everything from flaky to bizarre. There was little doubt that he had talent, but Hollywood directors and producers saw him mainly as an actor who was not mature enough for serious roles. Take a chance with Cage, the producers said, but only if there is an offbeat role to fill.

But before his breakthrough film *Leaving Las Vegas*, Cage began to alter his wild image. He has not left the offbeat behind,

A young Nicolas Cage costars with Kathleen Turner in Peggy Sue Got Married, *directed by Cage's uncle Francis Ford Coppola.*

but he has channeled his talents into more demanding roles that let his audiences and fans see the depths of his ability. Today, Nicolas Cage is one of Hollywood's top stars and leading men. He is respected for his talent and devotion to his craft, although he remains an unconventional figure and probably always will. As Cage himself says, "I've always tried to do the unexpected."[2]

Chapter 1

Destined for the Screen

A LIVELY IMAGINATION and a burning desire to act characterized the troubled childhood of Nicolas Cage, who struggled to control his anger and stand apart from his family's connections to the film industry. Born Nicolas Kim Coppola on January 7, 1964, he seemed destined for a career in the entertainment world if only because so much of his family was already involved in it.

Francesco Pennino, Cage's maternal great-grandfather, began the chain that would eventually link this Italian American family to the film industry. A pianist and songwriter, he arrived in the United States from Naples, Italy, during the early twentieth century. At first, he imported movies from Italy to be shown in America, which led to a job offer in Hollywood. Pennino declined and eventually played the piano for the great opera star Enrico Caruso. Cage's paternal grandfather, Carmine Coppola, was born in New York City and won a scholarship to Juilliard, the city's prestigious school of music and drama. At Juilliard, Coppola met Albert Pennino, Francesco's son. The two families were brought together when Carmine married Albert's sister Italia.

Cage's relatives were certainly made for the stage. Cage's mother, Joy Vogelsang Coppola, was a dancer and a choreographer. His aunt Talia Shire was nominated for an Academy Award for her performance as Connie Corleone in *The Godfather, Part 2* (1974). But Cage's most famous relative is his uncle

Francis Ford Coppola, the film director most notably known for *The Godfather* movies.

A Troubled Childhood

Cage's father, August Coppola, older brother to Francis and Talia, was the only immediate family member not involved in show business. Actually, August's father wanted him to be a doctor. Instead, Augie, as he was known, earned a doctorate in comparative literature and taught at the Long Beach campus of the California State University, near where Cage grew up. Augie also invented the tactile dome, an aid that helps blind people experience senses other than sight. A creative, sensitive man, Augie increasingly felt under pressure to compete with the growing fame and wealth of his brother Francis.

Cage's father, August "Augie" Coppola, was a professor of literature and the only family member not involved in the film industry.

The elder Coppola also felt overwhelmed with worry about his wife, Cage's mother. Talented and intense, Joy Coppola was often subject to bouts of depression. She was plagued with mental illness for most of Cage's childhood and was frequently institutionalized. Cage remembers, "She would go away for years at a time. When she got too erratic she went...away. Then my childhood consisted of going to see her. And that hallway [leading to her room] was a long hallway, let me tell you, going in there with the crazy people who would be touching and—it was very arresting."[3]

To treat her depression, Cage's mother underwent shock therapy. When she returned home after shock treatments, she had periods of relative calm and normalcy. Looking back on those times, Cage remembers his mother as a very gentle and sensitive person. For a while, life took on a normal middle-class existence for Cage and his two older brothers, Marc and Christopher. But as Cage grew older, his mother's periods of depression increased, as did her erratic behavior. She once told her husband that Nicolas was not his son but was born after an affair she had had with a well-known actor. Although Cage doubts the affair and apparently has no doubts about his father, Augie was so angered by the declaration that he became quite hostile to his youngest son in later years. As Cage explains, "The fact is if you look at a picture of my dad and you look at me, it's obvious that I'm his son. There has always been an edge from my father towards me and that must be the reason."[4]

As his mother's condition worsened and his father's frustration mounted, Cage often escaped into his own fantasy world. He had a highly active imagination and was content to live in his dream world for hours. The characters in his comic books sprang to life in his mind. He remembers sitting for long periods in front of the television set wanting to get inside the box where all those magic things were happening. His active imagination may have caused his nightmares about scary clowns, giant genies, and horrifying visions of human heads attached to cockroach bodies. He never shook his childhood fear of bugs.

Cage's imagination was further stimulated by movies. His father frequently took the Coppola boys to see film classics such

> ## The State of Depression
>
> Joy Coppola suffered from severe bouts of depression during Cage's childhood. Depression is probably the most common form of psychiatric complaint. It is marked by a state of extreme sadness, inactivity, and a reduced ability to enjoy life. Feelings of sadness or hopelessness often overwhelm the sufferer until he or she can no longer cope with everyday living. Feelings of sadness over the death of a loved one or the loss of a satisfying job do not necessarily indicate depression. But if such feelings do not abate in time or become severe, then the person is said to be suffering from depression.
>
> The three main treatments for diagnosed depression are psychotherapy, drug therapy, and shock treatments. Psychotherapy uses one-on-one contact with a therapist to try to resolve the underlying problems that may have caused the depressed state. Drug therapy corrects a chemical imbalance in the brain that might be causing the disorder. These two treatments are the most important in easing depression, but they were not effective for Coppola. Instead, she received the third treatment, electroconvulsive therapy, or shock treatments. An electric current is passed through the brain, which sometimes reduces the severe depressed state. The shock treatments enabled Cage's mother to come home for periods of time and function somewhat normally. During those periods, Cage felt that everything in his life was normal and hoped it might stay that way.

as *The Hunchback of Notre Dame* or *Phantom of the Opera*. Cage was fascinated with these movies, which inspired his interest in acting. By the time he was six years old, he was stealing clothes from his mother's wardrobe to dress up and play various parts. Although the three Coppola youngsters kept pretty much to themselves in their quiet middle-class neighborhood, they did sometimes put on plays they wrote for the neighbors. Cage remembers that he was especially good at disguising his voice, which became a useful talent to him as an actor. He was the star in the film epics shot by his brother Chris, who would later become a film director.

Cage used his acting skills at school as well as at home. Small and skinny, he was often picked on by the class bullies, but he found escape by being a clown and making them laugh. Sometimes he would go to school dressed as a cowboy or a monster. His antics amused his classmates and distracted the bullies. One particular bully in the fourth grade was so nasty that Cage had to come up with a clever way of evading him. One day Cage boarded the school bus dressed in one of his older brother's clothes, with his hair slicked back and wearing sunglasses. He told the bully that he was Nic Coppola's cousin and suggested that Nic better be left alone. It worked. Thinking back on his childhood, Cage later said that it was during these early years of pretending to be someone else that he learned he could act.

In school, Cage did not excel in any particular subject, so he made himself stand out in other ways. First, he tried to be a prankster to get attention. He was once expelled from elementary school for putting grasshoppers in egg salad sandwiches, which he gave to his classmates. Then he tried to be different. Sometimes he would wear one sleeve up and one down. Sometimes he boarded the school bus wearing a huge cowboy hat. Although he tried these things just to be unique, his teachers generally did not appreciate his antics. He did manage to get good grades, but he was frequently sent home with a note about his clownish behavior.

Augie had a hard time understanding why his youngest child was often in trouble at school, but for young Cage his antics seemed only natural. Besides, he liked to reinvent himself. If he saw a daredevil motorcycle rider on television, he would take his bike out in the backyard and try to jump over boxes. If he liked a particular actor, he would often imitate his speech or walk. When he was assigned a book to read in school, he imagined himself as the main characters. He remembers reading *Metamorphosis* by Franz Kafka, in which a young man wakes one morning to find he has been transformed into a repulsive insect. For a week after that, Cage walked around pretending to be a cockroach.

The Outsider

Cage's antics and disruptive behaviors at school were also a kind of escape from the often painful situation at home. His mother was frequently away. When she was home, she alternated between acting distant and loving. His parents also quarreled over raising the boys.

Finally, in 1976, when Cage was twelve years old, the situation at home changed dramatically when his parents divorced.

Beverly Hills High

The years that young Nicolas Cage spent at Beverly Hills High School (BHHS) in western Los Angeles were not among his happiest. Generally, he felt out of place in this suburban setting that has been the focus of movies and is said to contain one of the wealthiest high school populations in America.

Because of its location, near Hollywood, and its exceptional acting programs, it is not surprising that many Beverly Hills High students enter the movie industry after graduation. Actors Patrick Cassidy, Angelina Jolie, and Rob Reiner are BHHS graduates. Some graduates become involved in other areas of the entertainment industry. Christopher Lloyd, who produces the hit television show *Friends*; writer Nora Ephron; plus playwrights, concert violinists, and stars of the New York City opera have emerged from BHHS.

He remembers that time as both sad and good. It was sad because his mother wanted custody of the children but was not able to take care of them. It was good because it resolved the tension in the household caused by the friction between his parents.

Augie and the boys moved to a house on the outskirts of Beverly Hills that was still close enough to take advantage of the good school system. A four-year, college-oriented public school, Beverly Hills High serves a student body of about two thousand. High community support and some $7 million annually keep the academic standards and extracurricular offerings extremely high. Even so, the move was not a happy decision for Cage, for Beverly Hills High also boasts probably the richest students in the country.

Located in the center of the film industry and in a large metropolitan area, the school has a high percentage of students whose parents are in the entertainment world or are businesspeople such as lawyers and doctors. More than ever, Cage felt like an outsider. "I didn't like high school," he said. "I was a nerd and I didn't fit in."[5]

Name Recognition

By the time Cage attended high school, his uncle Francis Ford Coppola had become well known for directing the first two *Godfather* films (1972, 1974) plus *American Graffiti* (1973) and *The*

Conversation (1974). The *Godfather* movies, acclaimed as among the greatest American films ever, were two of the biggest moneymakers of all time, and both won the Academy Award for best picture. Coppola, who dropped the *Ford* from his name in 1979, was at the pinnacle of Hollywood fame. Since his uncle was so wealthy and well known, Cage felt poor in comparison, and the distraction bothered him a great deal. In fact, it would bother him until he became a success on his own. This feeling of inadequacy was enhanced by his own father's attitude about Francis. Augie always felt overshadowed by his fantastically successful younger brother.

Since Cage's last name was Coppola and the Coppola name was associated with fame and wealth, his classmates figured he

Perhaps best known for directing The Godfather *films, Francis Ford Coppola (right) supervises on* The Godfather Part III *set.*

was wealthy, too. They wanted to know why he was not driving a sports car, which most of the kids in Beverly Hills drove. Actually, Cage was not driving any car at all. Augie was trying to support three children on a teacher's salary and could not afford to buy cars for his sons.

The lack of a reliable car in Beverly Hills nearly wrecked Cage's prom night. After working odd jobs and saving money, he bought a sports car, a Triumph Spitfire, even though he did not have his driver's license yet. He would sit in the car in the driveway and pretend to be driving somewhere. What annoyed him most is that Augie sometimes drove it—and with the top down. But when Cage finally got his license, he discovered that his beloved car was unreliable and kept breaking down. Cage's way of handling frustration at that time was to get angry and take it out on things. One of his high school friends said he often drove into trash cans just to send them flying because he was so angry about his car troubles. So, when his car was not running on prom night, he had to rent a tuxedo plus a limo. He paid for both by cashing in a savings bond from his grandmother. However, at the prom he was so nervous when he kissed his date that he threw up on his shoes. The driver would not let him back into the limo, so he had to walk home.

Young Nicolas Cage was frustrated by being surrounded by so much money and social status, neither of which he himself had. Apparently so was his father, for Augie Coppola had his own problems dealing with his brother's wealth and fame. He even forbade Cage to see *The Godfather* when it was released. When Uncle Francis sent Cage some promotional T-shirts for the film, Augie threw them out. Cage did sneak out to a screening, however, and was deeply impressed with the performance of Al Pacino as Michael, the reluctant son of the Godfather who eventually takes over his father's position in the Corleone family. Cage thought Pacino was handsome and dramatic, and his forceful character was one Cage would like to portray on the screen. He especially admired Pacino's realistic portrayal of a young man torn between family loyalty and his own sense of right and wrong. Pacino achieved this realism through method acting, which Cage himself would later learn.

Al Pacino (left) appears with James Caan in a scene from The Godfather. *Cage idolized Pacino's powerful on-screen presence.*

Considering Augie's resentment of his brother's success, it must have been difficult for him to send his youngest son to live for a time with Uncle Francis on his $2-million Napa Valley ranch. Augie was making a lecture tour of the country and could not take Cage with him. With the older boys now out of school and away from home, Cage was sent into the affluent world of a successful show business personality. Although he was almost consumed with jealousy in his uncle's home, it did bring him to a decision about what he would do with his life. "I vowed then that I would go to Los Angeles, learn to act and then one day buy my own Victorian mansion in San Francisco. It was unfortunate," he said, "that it was revenge [on his uncle and his classmates] which fueled my ambition."[6]

Back in Beverly Hills

Even with his family background, the decision to become an actor was not going to be easy. Augie was against an acting career for his youngest son because he felt that the profession did

Destined for the Screen

not lead to a stable, worthwhile career. So when Cage returned to Beverly Hills High, he told his father he was joining the drama department because he wanted to become a writer. This pleased Augie and kept peace in the household.

While his father thought he was studying for a writing career, Cage was busy taking drama lessons in high school, where he acted in school plays, and at the Lee Strasberg School of Acting, which teaches method acting. Method actors immerse themselves into a role by developing a complete history for the character, such as mannerisms, beliefs, how he or she dresses, and even what the character eats. The founder, Strasberg, has strongly

Lee Strasberg founded the Lee Strasberg School of Acting and other groups where many noteworthy actors, like Cage, were trained.

The Lee Strasberg Schools

Cage attended the Lee Strasberg School of Acting, one of the most famous acting schools in the world. It was founded by Lee Strasberg, noted director, producer, actor, and teacher. In addition to the Lee Strasberg School, he founded several other groups to train actors, including the famous Group Theater and the Actor's Studio.

In 1966 a West Coast branch of Strasberg's Actor's Studio, where performers came to brush up on technique, was established in Los Angeles. Three years later, the Lee Strasberg Theatre Institute opened in New York. This made his work available to a wider public. From that, a Young People's Program was organized for teenagers and nonactors to help develop their creativity.

Strasberg died in 1982 at the age of eighty-one. Strasberg's great legacy comprises three generations of actors and playwrights. In addition, throughout his lifetime Strasberg strongly influenced countless directors and acting teachers.

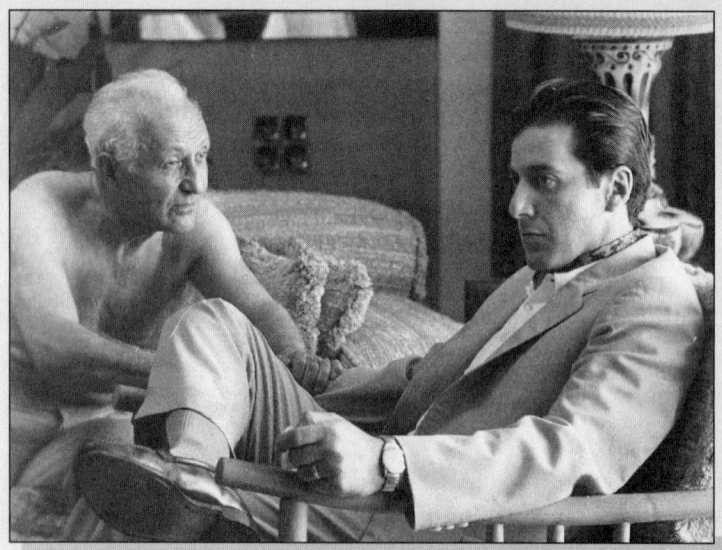

Strasberg (left) appeared with Al Pacino in The Godfather Part II.

influenced directors and acting coaches, and his permanent-cast theater has graduated some of America's most significant actors. Among them are Alec Baldwin, Paul Newman, Al Pacino, Jane Fonda, Marilyn Monroe, Jack Nicholson, James Dean, Dustin Hoffman, Steve McQueen, and Robert DeNiro. Cage longed to join the ranks of these talented method actors.

Cage fared well in the drama departments of both Beverly Hills High and Strasberg's school. He was highly active in the theater group, and one of his teachers later said he became the focal point of any scene in which he had a part. For the first time perhaps, Cage had finally found a place where he felt that he fit in. He was surrounded by people who had the dream of an acting career.

The drama school deception might have gone on indefinitely except that one night Cage was late returning home from an audition, and he told his father the truth. Augie was furious, screaming that his youngest son would never become an actor. For the only time that he can remember, Cage entered into a screaming match with his father, vowing that he would indeed follow an acting career. All the frustrations and anger of the past came back. Augie told Cage that he was not his son. And Cage accused his father of not doing enough to help his mother. It was a bitter moment from which their relationship never fully recovered.

After the argument with his father, Cage was more determined than ever to prove he could be a successful actor. But, to his great surprise, he was passed over for a featured role in the school's production of *West Side Story*. Suddenly, Cage made another decision. He was going to quit high school, although he was in his senior year. He believed he had the talent to make it on his own. School, he told his father, was just wasting his time. Augie was furious, but Cage would not give in. He simply refused to attend classes. He did, however, take and pass the General Educational Development test and later received his high school diploma.

The Short Career of Nicolas Coppola

Determined as he was to make it on his own, Cage was well aware that success would come more quickly if he traded on his family name. However, he could not bring himself to ask Uncle Francis for help. Instead, he told his father that he wanted to take a summer course at the American Conservatory Theatre in San Francisco. Perhaps Augie finally realized that his son was serious about an acting career, or perhaps he just wanted Cage to study something, so Augie agreed.

That summer Cage went to San Francisco, where his acting career began. He was cast in Clifford Odets's *Golden Boy*. This play, which was made into a movie in 1939, is the story of a young Italian American boxer. Instead of pursuing a career as a violinist, for which he has promising talent, he takes the faster way to fame in the boxing ring. Cage later said that portraying the boxer's powerful story made him feel like a real actor. Then a Hollywood manager named Chris Viores, who had seen Cage perform in high school, contacted him and suggested that he try out for television roles. At age seventeen, Cage won the part of a surfer on *The Best of Times*, a short-lived soap opera. But short as the series was, Cage's television role did cause the Coppola family, including Augie, to warm up a bit toward his career. They could see that he was determined to be an actor.

For his next tryout, Cage auditioned to play the role of Brad in *Fast Times at Ridgemont High* (1982), starring then unknown actor Sean Penn. Cage used his given name of Nicolas Coppola,

Sean Penn (pictured) became friends with Cage (then Nicolas Coppola) during the filming of the comedy Fast Times at Ridgemont High *in 1982.*

but he lost the part, although he did get the smaller role of Brad's buddy. *Fast Times* started as a best-seller by Cameron Crowe, a writer for *Rolling Stone* magazine. The movie tells of a year Crowe spent impersonating a student in a southern California high school, an atmosphere with which Cage was all too familiar.

Filming *Fast Times* was another learning experience for Cage. He got many acting tips from Penn during the production, and the two became good friends. At the same time, he endured many jokes from the rest of the cast about his name and how he got the part. The other actors were sure Cage was in the movie only because he was a Coppola. He suddenly felt the burden, he later said, of being Coppola's nephew. Having relatives in the movie business was proving to be a mixed blessing.

A Call from Uncle Francis

Yet when Uncle Francis called him to audition for the role of the bully Dallas in *The Outsiders* (1983), Cage accepted. The story is a highly stylized treatment of S. E. Hinton's best-selling novel concerning troubled teenagers in Oklahoma during the 1960s, as seen through the eyes of a boy.

Cage locked himself in a room for two weeks, drinking beer and staring at a picture of tough-guy movie actor Charles Bronson because he thought that would put him in the right mood to play a thug. However, Cage soon learned that he had been turned down for the part. Instead, Coppola suggested that his nephew play the lesser role of Two-Bit. The loss of the role so unnerved Cage that he frequently messed up his lines, and critics called his performance incompetent. He ended up in the hospital with a stress-induced illness. The experience led Cage to decide that he did not want to act after all.

After leaving the hospital and spending a few months selling popcorn in a movie theater, Cage changed his mind and decided that he did want to be an actor. But he had to change the odds against him. His family name was clouding other people's perceptions of his ability. In short, he had to change his name.

Changing names in Hollywood was a routine practice throughout most of the twentieth century. Studio heads wanted

Nicolas Cage is not the first actor to adopt a stage name. Actor Cary Grant (with Katharine Hepburn) was originally Archibald Alexander Leach.

actors who sounded less "ethnic" or just simply "more Hollywood." In that way, Julia Jean Mildred Frances Turner became Lana Turner, Frances Gumm was suddenly Judy Garland, Archibald Alexander Leach became Cary Grant, and Leonard Slye donned his cowboy hat to become Roy Rogers. Today, name changing still goes on, more likely if the name is too long to fit the screen, but it is less common because ethnicity is more acceptable.

Cage and his grandmother Divi, who also lived in the Hollywood area, sat down in her kitchen one night to think of a new name. Both of them liked Nicolas Vogel, a shortening of his mother's last name, but somehow that just did not sound right. Next, he decided on Nicolas Blue because it is his favorite color. Then he thought of keeping his ethnic heritage, so he came up with Nicolas Mascalzone, which means "scoundrel" in Italian. Cage may have liked the image, but his grandmother thought the name was too long and difficult to pronounce. After a few more suggestions, the pair picked Nicolas Cage. It was the last name of black superhero Luke Cage, Nicolas's favorite comic strip character, and Nicolas thought it symbolized escape, change, and freedom. It was also the last name of John Cage, Augie's favorite composer. Some years later, Cage commented that he now felt more like Nicolas Cage than Nicolas Coppola. His given name has become something from the past, tucked away along with his childhood memories.

The new name might have pleased Augie, but it did not please most of the other Coppolas. They regarded the change as a slur on their heritage. Coppola family members have never been shy about voicing their opinions. Said Cage's paternal grandmother, "It was a stupid, dumb jerk thing."[7] Uncle Francis, however, sent Cage a telegram of congratulations. Even better, he asked his nephew to be part of his upcoming film *Rumble Fish*. This time, Nicolas Cage, the actor, would succeed or fail with his own name.

Enter Nicolas Cage

Cage's career under his new name began with *Rumble Fish*. Originally, Coppola told his nephew that his job would be to audition other actors for the film. Actually, Coppola was sizing up Cage's acting ability against those auditioning. When Cage learned that he actually had a part in the movie, he could hardly believe it.

Rumble Fish (1983) is a kind of throwback to the James Dean rebel films of the 1950s. Coppola saw it as an art film for teenagers, filmed in high-contrast black and white. It is the story of two brothers, Rusty James (played by Matt Dillon), a cocky

Directed by Francis Ford Coppola, Rumble Fish *jumpstarted Cage's acting career with his role as Smokey (left).*

young man who lives in the shadow of his older brother. Cage plays Rusty's pal. Critic Leonard Maltin describes the movie as an "ambitious mood piece from S. E. Hinton's young-adult novel about [an] alienated teenager who lives in the shadow of his older brother. Emotionally intense but muddled and aloof."[8]

Rumble Fish was not much of a commercial success, but it did give Cage a start. Now he needed a starring role in a movie not directed by his uncle.

Chapter 2

Odd Man Out

FOR THE FIRST several years of his acting career, Nicolas Cage usually played such offbeat characters that he never seemed destined to be a Hollywood leading man. He did not deliberately set out to play weird roles, but his own personality seemed to embellish the parts. If the character was not already peculiar, Cage might add a strange walk or odd haircut or some gesture that set him apart. As an article in *American Film* notes,

> Nicolas Cage is not the star we expected, not from his generation, not in this day and age. Somebody forgot to blow-dry his hair, and the cowlick ended up in front. Somebody forgot to tell him that irony is hip, passion passé. Somebody forgot to smooth out that walk and that talk.... He's a character actor whose presence is frequently so powerful, it becomes part of the film's signature.[9]

Chest Hair and a Self-Centered Cad

Cage got his first professional starring role in *Valley Girl* in 1983. It was in this film that he first earned a reputation as an actor who would go to extraordinary lengths to understand the motivations of his character. In *Valley Girl* he plays Randy, a north Hollywood punk who meets a San Fernando girl, Julie, who has just broken up with her jock boyfriend. Julie has grown tired of her ex-boyfriend's arrogant attitude and becomes attracted to the mysterious Randy, whom she meets at the beach. With his strange hair and goofy looks, Randy is something different. To highlight the eccentricity of the character, Cage shaved some of

Cage's first starring role was that of Randy in Valley Girl.

his chest hair in order to form a V-shape that he thought made him look like Superman.

When he was not shaving his body hair, Cage could often be found participating in a different ritual, tattooing. Cage has an eight-inch-long lizard, complete with top hat and cane, tattooed on his back. He said his father turned white when he saw it. Cage feels that getting a tattoo is a bit like an initiation rite as one passes from boyhood to manhood.

After filming *Valley Girl*, Nicolas Cage, at age nineteen, was settling into the Hollywood life. He hired an agent, Ilene Feldman, although no one was clamoring for interviews. And at long last he bought a sporty car that really ran—a yellow Triumph Spitfire in which he cruised Sunset Boulevard.

Valley Girl received fairly good reviews. One critic said it was "several cuts above most contemporary teen pics."[10] And it got the industry talking about Nicolas Cage. Unfortunately, they were not talking about his acting ability but about how rather strange he was and how unusual he looked. Cage is six feet tall and has blue eyes under heavy lids, a crooked smile, and a brooding look most of the time. He walks with a sloping, fluid gait. Reviewers used phrases such as "hangdog expression" and "dopey sexuality"[11] to describe him. Cage did not mind the reviews; he just wanted to act.

His next chance came in 1984 with *Racing with the Moon*, a part he took mainly because it meant costarring with his friend Sean Penn, whom he much admires and considers to be inspirational. In this movie, Cage plays a self-centered cad who is about to join the U.S. Marines at the beginning of World War II. He learns that his girlfriend is pregnant and enlists the aid of his friend, played by Penn, to get money for an abortion. Some reviewers found the movie appealing and the performances of the two stars engaging, but it was not a big hit.

The Angry Young Actor

By 1984 Nicolas Cage had appeared in four films, but no one was taking notice. He was now twenty years old, an unconventional young man, a little on the wild side and with a great desire to be recognized. On the personal side, his mother's illness seemed to be improving with better medication, but his relationship with his father remained strained. Augie was now convinced that his son would be an actor, but he remained unhappy with the decision. Cage himself kept trying to impress his father with his maturity. After he got the lizard tattoo, for instance, he tried to explain to Augie that the act was a sign that he had become an adult and could make his own decisions.

Cage's next decision concerned his career. He accepted his uncle's offer of a role in *The Cotton Club* (1984). Although debating the wisdom of seeking another career boost from his uncle, Cage did feel that the part would enhance his status. Francis Coppola was still headline news. At the 1979 Cannes Film Festival he had won the Palme d'Or, the top prize at the acclaimed international film awards in France, for his *Apocalypse Now*, a controversial and cerebral film of a journey in war-torn Cambodia.

Cage's agent also had doubts about Cage appearing in *The Cotton Club*, declaring it would bring back all the old talk about family connections. It was almost a family movie; besides Cage,

Francis Ford Coppola

Cage's most famous family member is his paternal uncle Francis Ford Coppola, a Hollywood director known for *The Godfather* movies. Coppola, who was born in Detroit, Michigan, in 1939, was named for his maternal grandfather, Francesco Pennino, and for the *Ford Sunday Evening Hour*, a radio program that employed his father as an assistant conductor. Music and theater were part of Coppola's growing-up years, and he was most influenced by his visits to Radio City Music Hall in New York City after the family moved east. To him, these trips into the famed hall took on a magical quality because of the elegance of the theater itself and the talent he saw on the stage. He became interested in films at Hofstra University in New York and continued it at the University of California, Los Angeles, film school in 1960.

Coppola's name will always be linked to *The Godfather*, the first of the series, produced in 1972. Interestingly enough, this movie, considered by most critics to be one of the five greatest movies ever made, almost did not reach the silver screen in its final form. For one thing, a number of directors rejected the project before it reached Coppola. Marlon Brando, who plays the lead role, had been blacklisted (not wanted for his sometimes rebellious behavior) by Paramount Studios. After that was straightened out, Paramount also at first turned down Coppola's choice for the character Michael, who eventually takes over the role of Godfather. Coppola wanted Al Pacino, but the studio said he was too "Italian-looking" and too short. Eventually, Coppola got what he wanted, and the film became cinema history.

Coppola's success in Hollywood deeply affected his young nephew, Cage, in both positive and negative ways. Through his uncle, Cage was drawn to the theater and later made it his career. However, Coppola's great wealth and fame also made the boy feel inferior. As Cage later said, his own drive to succeed was partly a way of outshining his uncle.

Coppola's two sons, Gian-Carlo and Roman, were production assistants. Cage's acceptance of a role in *The Cotton Club* might promote the idea that he could only succeed in his acting career with the help of his famous relatives. However, Cage decided that despite the possible criticism of his family ties, his role in the movie was interesting enough to further his career.

The Cotton Club is Coppola's stylized look at the battle for control in Harlem, New York City, during the Prohibition era, when the sale of alcohol was against the law. It centers around the Cotton Club, a jazz place run by mobsters. Richard Gere is

Dixie, a cornet player at the club, and Cage plays his younger brother, Vincent "Mad Dog" Dwyer, who quickly finds his way onto the mobster's payroll as a professional goon.

The film, even with its wonderful soundtrack of Duke Ellington's music and its strikingly beautiful photography, was a disaster from the start. Early on, producer Robert Evans had trouble with finances for the movie. Although this was eventually settled, work on the movie was delayed. Then a feud between producer and director further complicated shooting. These delays were costly and frustrating for Cage. As Mad Dog Dwyer, complete with slicked-down hair and neatly trimmed mustache, he was hired for three weeks' work. That turned into six months of

Cage's slicked-down hair for his portrayal of Mad Dog Dwyer in The Cotton Club *was an authentic Prohibition-era style.*

filming at the same pay rate, during which time Cage could not look for or take on other roles. He was further frustrated by the fact that the movie was shot in New York City, an unfamiliar locale where he had no friends with whom to spend the off hours.

Enraged by the entire experience, Cage walked into his trailer one day and completely trashed it. He went berserk and threw a lamp and a pillow, among other things, out of his window. He then left his trailer and smashed a remote-controlled car that a city street vendor was selling. When Cage calmed down, he did pay for the car. However, people on the set thought he had lost his mind, and actor Richard Gere warned him that such outbursts could lead to a short career. As Cage says of that period, "[I was] behaving like a guy who listened to early Who music and wanted to be a rebel, a punk rocker, an outlaw of some sort, and didn't really know how to act. I don't need to do that now, but because I went through that period, it still comes back to bite at me sometimes."[12]

The Brat Pack

At this point in his career, during the early to mid-1980s, Cage was associated with—although never a full member of—a group of young Hollywood types known as the Brat Pack. The 1960s had the Rat Pack, which included established, well-known, and often rowdy stars such as Frank Sinatra, Dean Martin, and Sammy Davis Jr., who generally acted outlandishly around town and made headlines doing so. The 1980s marked a hopeful decade for Hollywood. During the 1970s, production costs had soared in the film industry, but ticket sales declined. Cable television cut into the industry as well. But the 1980s changed that situation. A number of mergers and takeovers greatly increased profits.

Into this new setting came a small group of young stars, known as the Brat Pack, who began to dominate the youth-oriented films of the decade. Names such as Emilio Estevez, Rob Lowe, Demi Moore, Sean Penn, and Molly Ringwald began to appear. These young actors were mostly born during the 1960s, as was Cage, and they became the darlings of Hollywood. Unlike the Rat Pack, most of them had grown up in the movie

Odd Man Out

During the 1980s, Cage was associated with many Brat Pack actors (pictured), although he never considered himself a part of the group.

industry and were often disdainful of it. They starred in films that, for the most part, talked of wealth, status, and conformity. Their performances came to represent the dreams of teens and young people across the country, and their not-very-private lives filled the movie magazines.

Although Cage sometimes hung out with the Brat Pack on their nightclub jaunts around town, he never considered himself truly a part of the group. He regarded himself as a rebel, more of the Marlon Brando image. Regarded as one of the greatest of Hollywood actors, Brando became a leading man in 1947, and in his early films he portrayed the rebellious nonconformist who strutted about the stage in defiance of authority. Cage was more into motorcycles and tattoos than going to nightclubs and wearing trendy T-shirts, which the Brat Pack favored. In addition, he seemed to be the only one of the group who had accepted the

Following in Brando's Footsteps

For a time, Nicolas Cage fancied himself as a Marlon Brando type of actor. Best known today for his starring role in *The Godfather*, Brando was one of Hollywood's hottest stars and a pronounced rebel during the 1950s. He impressed Broadway in 1947 as Stanley Kowalski, a surly character who picks fights, in Tennessee Williams's *A Streetcar Named Desire*.

His motorcycle-riding character in *The Wild One* (1954) enhanced his reputation as a rebel. Nominated for an Academy Award four times, Brando won his second Oscar for the title character in *The Godfather* (1972). He caused a sensation at the celebration by refusing the award in order to protest the plight of Native Americans and the way they are portrayed in movies.

Brando's reputation impressed the young actor Cage. In a time when Hollywood's leading men were neatly dressed and sophisticated, Brando wore t-shirts and had tattoos. He played the uneducated, almost boorish, often angry young man who fought against the pain of living in a world where he did not fit in. Cage understood the kind of anguish and rebellious feelings that Brando brought to his films.

Marlon Brando portrayed angry "bad boys" in such early films as On the Waterfront *(pictured) and* The Wild One. *Cage admired his work in these roles.*

fact that an actor could make a living playing character roles rather than as a star.

Teeth Out and Shirt Off

His search for another good character role led Cage to *Birdy*, also in 1984. In this film, Cage plays a shell-shocked Vietnam War veteran named Al, who is trying to recover from his war experiences. Doctors bring him to the bedside of his childhood friend Birdy (Matthew Modine), who is hospitalized for postwar trauma. Birdy cannot talk, but he fantasizes about birds in flight, an obsession that has haunted him since childhood. Al tries to coax Birdy away from his hallucinations. The movie is presented mostly in stark flashbacks told from Al's point of view, and it emphasizes the mental results of war and the power of friendship.

Cage really exhibited his mastery of method acting in this film. Wanting to experience some of the pain of his facially injured character, he had his wisdom teeth pulled out as the shooting started. He felt that the pain would make him feel more like a physically maimed veteran. However, he denies all rumors that it was done without novacaine for more realism. Although the movie was not a great audience pleaser, it won the Grand Jury Prize at the Cannes Film Festival, the first award for a film featuring Nicolas Cage.

There was little critical praise for Cage's next movie appearance, *The Boy in Blue* (1986). In this film, Cage portrays the nineteenth-century Canadian rowing champ Ned Hanlan. For this role, he wore a fake tan and built up real muscles since most of the movie involves Cage walking around without a shirt. He did not like the "hunk look," and audiences did not like it either. Cage says that he learns from mistakes that he makes in his movies. Of this film, he later commented, "When I saw that [*The Boy in Blue*], I said, Well, I'm never going to take my shirt off again—at least not like that. I wanted to get as far as I could from the beefcake image."[13] *New York Times* movie critic Nina Darnton did not comment on his image but rather on his acting: "He doesn't infuse the role with the kind of personal depth or individual detail that would make the character come alive."[14]

Playing the Character

Cage tried so much to make the character in his next movie come alive that he was nearly tossed off the set—at the request of his costar. *Peggy Sue Got Married* (1986) was another film directed by Coppola, and Cage's uncle blamed him for the trouble that followed.

The story centers around Peggy Sue (Kathleen Turner), a forty-three-year-old, about-to-be-divorced former prom queen who travels back in time to her senior year in high school. From there she views what a failure her life has become. Her small-town husband, Charlie (Cage), is having an affair and their marriage is falling apart. As she relives her teenage years, she sees the decisions made then that brought her to the current state. Some of the movie's appeal is the look at a bygone era, such as

Cage was nearly fired for his outlandish interpretation of the role of Charlie in Peggy Sue Got Married.

> **Method Acting**
>
> Method acting, which originated with Lee Strasberg, has been taught by his widow, Anna, and by other adherents since his death. In this form of acting, actors develop a complete life history for their character in order to understand the character's motives and beliefs. Anna Strasberg claims that the main ingredient in method acting is honesty. She says her husband never taught an actor how to act; he only taught actors how to live in a truthful way. It is possible for an actor, Anna believes, to live truthfully under imaginary circumstances. Method acting has been compared to ballet exercises. Just as the initial minutes of exercise at the ballet bar are basically the same everywhere, the same set of method acting exercises allows an actor free range in anything from Shakespeare to a television sitcom. It takes the basics of the craft of acting to their highest level.
>
> Method acting comes under constant reevaluation. Some acting teachers wonder if the memory exercises that are used are really the best way to prepare an actor for a performance. Some suggest they are merely a gimmick that turns an actor into an amateur psychiatrist trying to get in touch with his or her inner self and specific emotions. Nonetheless, some of Hollywood's best and brightest are true believers in this way of bringing a character to life on the stage or screen.

Peggy Sue's father extolling the virtues of his new car, an Edsel, which was the lemon of the late 1950s.

Turner plays the part not as the people around her see her, but as she sees herself, whereas Cage plays Charlie as others see him. He portrays Charlie as a stylized version of an early 1960s teenager. Cage came on the set wearing a platinum wig with a high pompadour (poofed up hair in the front) and buck teeth. In the movie, he speaks in a nasal twang voice and acts totally silly.

Some critics actually found something in Charlie that was touching, but Turner became hysterical. She shouted that Cage was making a mockery of the film. The producers were outraged, and even Coppola wondered what was going on. Everyone wanted Cage fired and off the set. Cage later admitted that if his uncle had not been directing, he certainly would have been fired. It took lots of placating and many pasta dinners served to the producers for Coppola to keep the production moving. Coppola also promised that some of the gestures and antics that Cage put into his role would be toned down in the cutting room.

They were not. Critic Leonard Maltin thought the movie was wistful and Turner had star-radiant power, but "Cage's annoying performance as the boyfriend is another debit."[15] Critic Mark Rowland said in his article, "[Cage] turned his part into a romantic goofball, one not unlike—and perhaps inspired by—Jerry Lewis in *The Nutty Professor*."[16] Cage later said he thought his interpretation of the character would be entertaining to everyone, but obviously he was wrong.

The Down Side

To no one's surprise, Nicolas Cage was not Hollywood's most popular actor after his performance in *Peggy Sue Got Married*. His uncle was still annoyed with him. Most of the critics thought he was too bizarre to bother with. And his personal life was not doing too well either. Cage dated many young women during his early career, but for the past three years he had been involved with Jenny Wright, a regular on the soap opera *General Hospital*. Now the relationship was showing signs of strain. His career and his personal life seemed to be going nowhere.

For the first time since his hospital visit following *The Outsiders*, Cage began to have real doubts about his chosen profession. He wondered if his method acting and somewhat unconventional demeanor were doing him more harm than good. Oddly enough, it was that unconventional demeanor that secured his next movie role.

Raising Expectations

Cage's ninth film, *Raising Arizona* (1987), was a perfect match between producers and star, and it fit the young actor's image. Filmmaking brothers Joel and Ethan Coen also had a reputation for the offbeat. They had ridden to some success with their made-on-a-shoestring cult flick *Blood Simple* (1984), about a husband who hires a slimy character to kill his wife and her boyfriend. Although it was critically acclaimed, it made little money, so the brothers decided on a lighter pace for their next production.

This time the Coens chose a frantic farce that takes usual stereotypes in new directions. H.I. McConnough (played by

Odd Man Out

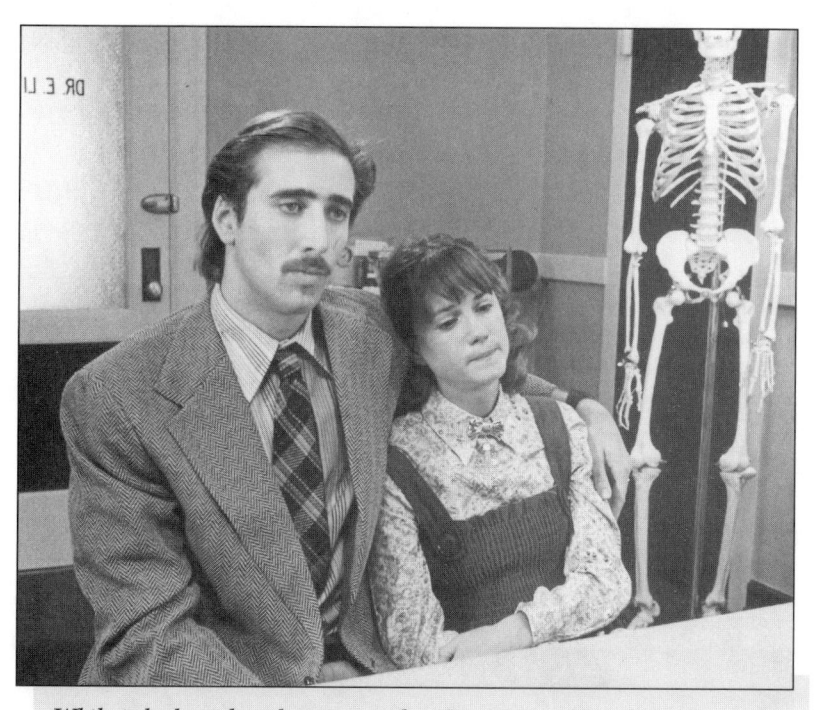

While it had weakened previous roles, Cage's unconventional acting style was a perfect match for the offbeat Raising Arizona.

Cage) is an armed robber who falls in love with Edwina, the policewoman (Holly Hunter) who has arrested him. They decide to get married once he swears to end his robbing ways. Then they find out they are unable to have children, and with H.I.'s past record, they cannot adopt. The solution seems quite easy to them when they decide to kidnap one of a set of quintuplets born to Mr. and Mrs. Arizona. They reason that the parents will not miss the child because they already have so many. Once they have the child, it is obvious they have no idea what to do with him. So follows the dizzying plot, which does not always make sense but is fun for audiences.

After casting Hunter as the wife, the Coens were hung up on casting just the right actor to play the flaky husband. Then they saw Nicolas Cage in *Peggy Sue Got Married*, and they knew they had found their man. It was a match made in Hollywood heaven. Cage loved the script at first reading. "The first contact I had with the film was through the script," he said, "and I was sold as soon as I read it. I was impressed with it because it required no adjustments."[17]

Whatever success came to *Raising Arizona*, and there was much, can in large part be credited to the Coen brothers. For the first time in Cage's career, directors were able to rein in his wild inclinations and keep him on track. Cage went to the set full of ideas on how the character should be played, how he should talk, how he should look. He was prepared to improvise as he had done in his earlier films, but the Coens had their own ideas. Joel Coen, who directed, was as firm about what he wanted from the character as Cage was about how he thought the role should be played. The director won, and Cage suddenly

The Coen brothers (pictured) harnessed Cage's wild persona to make Raising Arizona *a success.*

found that it was sometimes an advantage to listen to advice about how a role might be played.

The result was an absurd film that was not to everyone's taste but that won kudos from many critics. Peter Reiher, who did not like the movie overall, says,

> There are several funny moments...and Nicolas Cage...gives an excellent performance. His character is a dimwitted rube who's not very strong on honesty, but Cage makes him lovable, rather like a large, stupid dog whose misdeeds are so inept as to make you feel sorry for him. Cage's greatest achievement is that he makes H.I. seem like a real person.[18]

Pauline Kael, a critic for the *New Yorker*, writes, "Cage has sometimes been expected to carry roles that he wasn't ready for, but his youth works for him here."[19]

People really noticed Nicolas Cage after his performance in *Raising Arizona*, but he was right back where he started—a somewhat bizarre actor with a lot of talent. His fan base was growing, but to the average Hollywood producer, Cage was still not someone to take a chance on for an important starring role. A famous name, a gutsy director, and a delightful comedy would start to change that image.

Chapter 3

Toward a New Image

STARTING WITH *MOONSTRUCK* in 1987, Nicolas Cage began to project a new image that would eventually change his status in Hollywood. Although he later admitted that he did not even want to do the movie at first and he did not realize its potential, *Moonstruck* showed fans and producers a more versatile, mature side of the actor. He would continue to fall back on the old familiar roles, but this movie marked a turning point for his screen image. As Cage later said, "I don't think I was mature enough to know it or to tell anybody at the time. The film was my first blockbuster."[20]

A Gem of a Movie

Audiences and critics alike considered *Moonstruck*, starring Oscar-winner Cher, to be a four-star gem of a movie, its magical quality reflected in the title. Directed by Norman Jewison, the film is a romantic comedy about an Italian American family living in New York City. Cher plays Loretta Castorini, a bored thirty-eight-year-old widow who, more out of weariness than love, is about to marry boring-but-dependable Johnny Cammareri (Danny Aiello). When Johnny travels to Sicily to see his dying mother, Loretta meets his younger brother, Ronny (played by Cage), to invite him to the wedding. The two brothers have not talked to each other for years. While Loretta's fiancé lingers in Italy, Loretta and Ronny fall passionately in love—struck, it is said, by the moonlight. The resolution of their romantic problems, plus the effect of the moon on all the characters, results in a film that exudes laughter and warmth.

Moonstruck was a big hit with audiences and with critics. According to Roger Ebert of the *Chicago Sun-Times*, "The movie is filled with fine performances...by Cage as the hapless, angry brother, who is so filled with hurts that he has lost track of what caused them. In its warmth and in its enchantment, as well as in its laughs, this is the best comedy in a long time."[21]

However, the movie had a decidedly rocky beginning. Cage initially did not want the part in *Moonstruck*, and director Jewison did not want him either. Cage admitted he was still looking for something wild and unconventional. Jewison admitted that he thought Cage's reputation for bizarre behavior, such as his antics on the set of *Peggy Sue*, would ruin his film. Neither of them had counted on what Cher wanted.

When Cher had signed on to star in the film, the part of Ronny had not yet been cast. When she saw *Peggy Sue Got Married*, she decided that Nicolas Cage was the ideal Ronny. Both director Jewison and the movie's producers promptly vetoed the idea, shocked that she would even suggest anyone with such a reputation. They were not going to have Cage ham up the role and ruin this film as he had done for *Peggy Sue*, they said. But

Cher and Nicolas Cage star in the 1987 hit, Moonstruck. *Cage originally did not want to be a part of this more conventional film.*

Cher is one of Hollywood's top stars, and such a celebrity usually gets what she wants. Jewison and the producers finally hired Cage, but they were far from happy.

As for Cage, he credits Cher with giving his career a significant boost. At first he could not believe that as a young actor, now age twenty-three, he had the chance to play opposite one of Hollywood's most powerful stars. "Cher was a champion for me," he said later. "I didn't want to do the movie at first. I wanted to do some punk movie, some wild, rebellious gesture. It's only now that I look back and realize how lucky I was."[22]

Even after Cher assured his part in the movie, director Jewison took no chances on any of Cage's well-publicized antics. He insisted that Cage do a screen test even though he had already been chosen for the part. Jewison wanted to know beforehand just how Cage saw the role; he did not want any changes on the set. Although this role was a big boost for Cage, his temperament remained pretty much the same. Director and actor inevitably ended up in conflict, with Jewison insisting on his way and Cage screaming at the top of his lungs when he disagreed. Cage once threw a chair across the stage during a confrontation. In fact, for a time it looked as though Cage might be thrown off the set of *Moonstruck* as well. As he became more familiar with the role, he began to think of Ronny as having a more "beastlike," darker side than the script envisioned. Jewison, although he has high respect for Cage as an actor, was opposed to any change in the interpretation of Ronny's character. There were many tense moments, but in general Jewison succeeded in controlling any excesses in Cage's behavior for the benefit of the film.

Despite their differences, Jewison did have a good deal of praise for Cage's final performance:

> As the film progresses Nicolas blossoms into a classic romantic leading man—I think it was the first film where he'd come off that way.... He took unbelievable chances as an actor. Every time I got angry with him I'd just look in his eyes.... You knew he would be willing to give anything and everything a chance, in love and work—in anything. He was a gambler.[23]

The Gambler in Love

The filming of *Moonstruck* and the end of his affair with Jenny Wright left Nicolas Cage a changed man. The film made him a movie star and gave him a reputation as a leading man. He was suddenly a millionaire. Now he could afford the sports cars and motorcycles that he loved, spending much of his time driving

A Cage Kind of Car

Nicolas Cage has probably never met a sports car he did not like. One of his favorites is the Italian-made Ferrari, which often dominated world racing competitions during the second half of the twentieth century. Enzo Ferrari, a car manufacturer, designer, and racing driver from Modena, Italy, joined the Alfa Romeo Company as a driver in 1920. In 1937 he designed his first racing car for the company. Two years later he left Alfa Romeo to found Ferrari SpA, but he did not manufacture his own automobiles until after World War II. Before long, the Ferrari became known for its great speed and exceptional handling quality. The Ferrari Formula One racer won many a competition from the 1950s on. Enzo Ferrari sold 50 percent of his company to Fiat SpA in 1969 but remained president until 1977. He retained control of the Ferrari racing cars until his death in 1988. Today, the Ferrari is a symbol of wealth and grand living.

Cage is enamored of sports cars, particularly Ferraris. The version of the Ferrari used by professional race-car drivers is pictured here.

around Hollywood to show off his new toys. In his personal behavior, he changed little. He still felt like a rebel on the wild side, and he still had a temper that erupted when things displeased him.

To befit his new status as a celebrity, Cage decided to buy a home. He chose a 1928 gothic-style castle in Loz Feliz in the Hollywood Hills. Cage, who has never been embarrassed about spending money lavishly, purchased the house for $1.5 million. He decorated his new home with a velvet sofa, carved gargoyles, stuffed black beetles, and a six-foot-tall metal fly. He says it was always his dream as a child to live in a castle.

In addition to the new home, cars, motorcycles, and celebrity status, Cage was also now a very eligible and rich bachelor. Hollywood's young, rich crowd frequented a hip eatery called Canter's, and that became Cage's favorite nightspot. It was there that he met his future wife, Patricia Arquette.

When Arquette, who was nineteen years old at the time, walked by Cage in Canter's one night, he told her that they would marry one day. According to one reporter, "She told him he was crazy, but played along with him when he asked her to give him a list of 'impossible' things he had to get in order to win her love."[24] Arquette's "impossible" wish list was a black orchid, an autograph from famed writer J. D. Salinger, and a large fiberglass statue from Bob's Big Boy, a hamburger restaurant chain. She thought she had seen the last of Cage.

However, Cage had fallen instantly in love, so he refused to let the impossible wishes deter him. The next day Arquette found an autographed Salinger letter, which reportedly cost Cage one thousand dollars or more in an autograph shop, on her doorstep. The following day he drove up on his motorcycle with a purple orchid that he proceeded to spray-paint black. He told her that he was going after the Big Boy statue that night, but Arquette stopped him by saying she would go away with him somewhere, but they were not going to marry. They spent the next three weeks together roaming Mexico. During that period, Arquette saw the disturbing side of Cage's personality—his temper. Reacting to a mix-up in tickets at the airport, he threw one of his legendary tantrums. When they returned to Los An-

> **Another Entertainment Family**
>
> When Nicolas Cage met Patricia Arquette, he learned that the woman he called his soulmate also was the product of a show-business family. Her grandfather was Cliff Arquette, who was Charley Weaver on the popular *Hollywood Squares* television game show. Arquette is also the daughter of actor Lewis Arquette and the sister of actors David, Rosanna, Richmond, and Alexis.
>
> Born in Chicago in 1968, Arquette got her career start in television but began acting in films in 1987 with the third *A Nightmare on Elm Street*. Besides her one movie with Cage, she is best known for her gutsy portrayal of Alabama in the hip action film *True Romance* and for her tender role in *Ethan Frome* (both 1993). Arquette says that she likes playing a goody-two-shoes role in one film and someone bold and erotic in the next. It is what she finds most exciting about being an actress.
>
> *Nicolas Cage's first wife, actress Patricia Arquette, also hails from a show business family.*

geles, Arquette decided not to continue the relationship. Although they did not see each other for the next eight years, they frequently talked on the telephone.

The Bug Diet

Unhappy over his failed romance, Cage threw himself into a series of rocky and unstable relationships. Finally, he began an affair with actress/model Christina Fulton, and she moved into his castle.

Cage also threw himself into his work, but he chose films that put him right back where he was before *Moonstruck*, playing the odd character once again and immersing himself deeply in such roles, as when he played a vampire in a horror movie. *Vampire's Kiss* (1989) is the story of Peter Lowe (Cage), a successful New York literary agent who thinks he has been bitten by a vampire. His therapist, however, does not believe him, even though he keeps out of the light, avoids crosses, and wears fake fangs. It was not a movie destined to make Hollywood producers seek out Cage as a leading man. It certainly was not a movie that his agent or advisers wanted him to make. Yet Cage as usual was going his own way. "Cage's conversation-piece performance is so over the top that it's conceivable the actor was bitten in real life. Amusing at times, also tasteless,... but whatever your feelings about the content, Cage is really something to see,"[25] said one critic.

Today, Cage admits that he may never live down the reputation he built for himself during the filming of *Vampire's Kiss*. He became so deeply immersed in the vampire role that his coworkers noticed him thinking and acting "like a vampire" on the set. For example, while shooting a scene where a bat appears, Cage wanted to use a real live bat instead of a mechanical one. That was not possible—even if the director, Robert Bierman, would have allowed it—because using a live bat on the set is against the law. As Cage's character descends into madness, he is supposed to eat raw eggs in one scene. Instead, Cage decided to eat a live cockroach despite his fear of bugs. He says he got the idea from the original 1931 version of *Dracula*, in which the vampire's servant runs around the castle catching live insects for dinner.

Audience reaction to Cage's cockroach consumption was intense to say the least. At the time all the fuss seemed to annoy Cage. At the time, he said, "My whole take on that cockroach is that I saved the movie hundreds of thousands of dollars in special effects,... and all I did was eat a bug."[26] Today, Cage admits it was an awful experience and it still makes him sick thinking about it.

Fatherhood

About the time that *Vampire's Kiss* was completed, Cage's expenses on his castle were rising. He decided that he needed more money, so he agreed to star in a helicopter movie called *Fire Birds* (1990). Once again he went against the advice of his agent, who felt the film was not for him.

Britain's David Green directed this high-tech tale, costarring Tommy Lee Jones, about U.S. pilots in their $10-million-apiece army helicopters battling drug lords in South America. This time, the whirlybird action far overshadowed the characters, which was not good for Cage, whose stage presence usually dominates the screen. Critics also complained that there was no chemistry between Cage and female lead Sean Young. It was both a critical and a financial flop.

During the filming of *Fire Birds*, Cage appeared more irritable and quarrelsome than usual on the set. Perhaps that was

Cage plays a literary agent who believes he is turning into a vampire in Vampire's Kiss. *Cage ate a live cockroach for his performance in the film.*

because he had just received some unexpected news from his girlfriend, Fulton: He was going to be a father. He worried that now he would need more money than ever. He and Fulton also had to make a decision about their future. It took them weeks to talk things over, but Cage and Fulton finally decided that their commitment to each other was not strong enough for marriage. However, they would continue to live together and raise their son. Weston Coppola Cage was born on December 26, 1990.

More on the Wild Side

After *Vampire's Kiss* and before the birth of his son, Cage found a movie that the director thought, based on Cage's past reputation, was a perfect role for him. *Wild at Heart* (1990) is the dark, violent tale of Sailor Ripley, a psychotic drug addict. He embarks on a cross-country journey with his girlfriend, Lula Fortune, whose mother has sent a hitman after them to kill Sailor. The movie is so violent that it nearly qualified for an X rating. It contains so many weird characters on the road trip that Cage's portrayal of Sailor seems almost normal in comparison.

Cage loved the part of Sailor because it gave him a chance once again to come up with a personal interpretation of the character. This time he had no argument from director David Lynch. In fact, Cage was the director's first and only choice for the part. Lynch liked the actor's wild, offbeat nature, perhaps because the director had a reputation for the offbeat himself. He agreed when Cage decided to infuse the role with Elvis Presley–like characteristics. Cage mumbles with an Elvis-like accent and even sings in a parody of the star. The movie took the top prize at the Cannes Film Festival, but back home the reviews were not so glowing. Roger Ebert wrote, "The movie is lurid melodrama, soap opera, exploitation, put-on and self-satire. Cage looks like a villain in a silent movie and does a conscious imitation of Presley in all of his dialogue."[27]

After *Wild at Heart*, Cage reached a point where he felt satisfied with his career. Perhaps he just was not destined for the leading-man roles. By this time, he had a small but ardent fan base that reveled in his antics. Due to the success of his latest film, he had lots of money to spend again. He had also estab-

Nicolas Cage kisses Laura Dern in Wild at Heart. *The film almost received an X rating for its extremely violent scenes.*

lished a lifestyle that allowed him to indulge in wild, often inappropriate behavior.

Cage's wild behavior became news on July 20, 1990. He was on a commuter flight from Los Angeles to San Francisco, and he had too much to drink. Somehow he got control of the public address system and announced that the captain was sick and about to lose control of the plane. When he was met by police at San Francisco's airport, he explained he was bored and thought it was funny. No one else did, especially not the Federal Aviation Authority, which could have brought civil charges against him. He was let off with a stern warning, relieved that he had not been jailed.

Maybe it was the realization that he could have gone to jail that made Nicolas Cage take stock of his private and professional lives in 1990. Maybe it was that event coupled with the birth of his son, which Cage says greatly affected his life. As he said later about fatherhood, "It brings a new kind of emotion, a new depth that wasn't there before. I'm always aware that what I do could affect my son.... Being a father has had more of an impact on my life than anything else before or since."[28] Although he and Fulton remained friends, they finally parted. They agreed on shared custody of their son. On nights when Fulton was caring for Weston, Cage could generally be seen at Hollywood nightclubs, an attractive young starlet on his arm.

As for his professional life, this was another unsure period. He felt he should make changes, yet part of him remained somewhat defiant about what roles he should pursue and how the characters should be portrayed. Part of him wanted to bring Nicolas Cage the actor into the Hollywood mainstream.

The Comedy Roles

As a path to the mainstream, Cage thought he might give lightness and comedy a chance. He says,

> I saw that always trying to shock was an adolescent state of mind. I realized that I did not have to be that kind of guy to be cool or prove I wasn't a nerd. Plus, I sensed that I'd almost worn out my welcome as this dark, rebellious image. That's why I made what I refer to as my "sunshine trilogy"—*Honeymoon in Vegas* (1992), *It Could Happen to You* (1994), and *Guarding Tess* (1994).[29]

In the first of the so-called sunshine trilogy, *Honeymoon in Vegas*, Cage seems comfortable with this lighter kind of comedy, which is less frantic than *Raising Arizona*. He plays Jack Singer, who elopes to Las Vegas to marry his true love, Betsy (Sarah Jessica Parker). Jack gets involved in a card game with a mobster (James Caan) who has fixed the game. When Jack gets an unbelievable hand and then loses and cannot pay the money, he is told the debt will be cleared if Betsy spends a weekend with the mobster. A horrified Betsy goes off with the mobster, and Jack spends the rest of the movie tracking them down.

Honeymoon in Vegas is a farce and nonsense. As one reviewer observes, "This is all played for laughs, and it's great fun... in

Cage poses with Sarah Jessica Parker and James Caan for Honeymoon in Vegas, *a comedy that boosted Cage's appeal.*

the hands of Caan and Cage, it still works marvelously well.... Ridiculous as it seems, we can somehow believe these events might happen."[30] It does, however, stretch even the believable at times. For instance, as the movie ends, a flood of Elvis Presley look-alikes skydive along with Cage's character, and Cage once again impersonates Presley. Perhaps because of the nonsensical storyline, a number of critics panned both the movie and Cage's comedy act.

Despite the critics' opinions, *Honeymoon in Vegas* was good for Cage because it gave him some mass-appeal recognition. Audiences thought he was funny. In fact, the movie brought him a Golden Globe nomination as best actor in a comedy or musical.

With steady work, Cage now had lots of money to spend on his castle and on cars. He no longer purchased motorcycles. Instead, he collected cars: a silver Peugeot convertible formerly owned by Dean Martin, a Ferrari, a 1967 Chevelle, a 1967 Corvette Stingray coupe, a Lamborghini, and a black Porsche.

While spending his money and looking for another lighter, more mass-appeal part, Cage appeared in three movies for which he received little pay: *Red Rock West, Amos and Andrew,* and *Deadfall.* All three were mainly forgettable.

Cage's first return to the mass-appeal market since *Moonstruck* occurred in 1994, and critics and audiences applauded two out of his three films that year. In *Guarding Tess,* Cage is Secret Service agent Doug Chesnick, who has been guarding former First Lady Tess Carlisle (Shirley MacLaine) in Sommersville, Ohio. Now, Chesnick is not happy to be told that he is back at the same job for another three years—at Tess's request. What follows is a comedic war of wills, and the reviewers felt that most of it worked. Reviewer James Berardinelli says, "Nicolas Cage carries the movie. Normally known for his manic on-screen antics, it's interesting to see Cage in a restrained performance."[31]

Whenever Cage has appeared in a so-called restrained performance, reviewers and colleagues alike have commented on the feeling of harnessed emotion he exhibits. To the audience, he is holding himself in, but there is a sense of turmoil just beneath the surface. In his best roles, this awareness of energy waiting to

Critics and audiences celebrated Cage's portrayal of a Secret Service agent protecting a former first lady (Shirley MacLaine) in Guarding Tess.

break free is captivating and often holds an audience spellbound even when the rest of the film or the cast is lacking.

Critics found Cage extremely likeable in the romantic comedy *It Could Happen to You* (1994), based on a true-life story that occurred in the small Hudson River town of Dobbs Ferry, New York. This movie reunited him with Andrew Bergman, director of *Honeymoon in Vegas*. Cage plays Charlie Lang, a good-guy cop who shares his lottery ticket with a hard-luck waitress (Bridget Fonda) because he does not have the money to leave her a tip. The ticket wins and they become millionaires. The role of Lang was a world away from vampires, and Cage said he played his nice-guy character as almost too good to be true because that is what Lang was. According to critic Maltin, "Warm, winning performances by Cage and Fonda carry this N.Y.-based fairy tale."[32]

Good-bye Comedy

It began to look as though Cage had found a niche in the romantic comedy business. Then along came *It Happened in Paradise* (1994) and the warm, romantic comedy niche disappeared.

Even Cage did not like the film, although that was probably because it was filmed in Canada during one of the country's coldest winters ever. He certainly gained no warmth from the movie critics, who generally found the comedy about a bank robbery in a small town anything but funny. Cage thought its original title, *Trapped in Paradise*, better reflected the picture.

In addition to his dissatisfaction with the movie, Cage's personal life was in turmoil. Yet another relationship had failed. Cage withdrew from the nightclub circuit, spending time alone in his castle in the Hollywood Hills. Being alone gave Cage

In the real-life story It Could Happen to You, *Cage plays a New York cop who splits his lottery ticket winnings with a waitress.*

> ### The La Brea Tar Pits
> One of Cage's favorite places in Southern California is the La Brea Tar Pits in Hancock Park, Los Angeles. *La Brea* means "the tar" in Spanish, and the site earned the name because its springs ooze crude oil. The pits are fossil-bearing and contain the skulls and bones of entrapped prehistoric animals and fossilized plants. Exhibits in the park itself show giant lifesize figures of long-extinct creatures as well as an observation pit. During Cage's early career, he would often sit on a park bench outside the tall chain-link fence that guards the pits. He likes to look at the watery pool that ripples with methane bubbles coming up from cracks in the earth. Cage says it gives him a sense of what prehistoric times must have been like—full of sea monsters and sea serpents.

more time to pursue his interests, such as decorating his home. From time to time there were reports of some of the furnishings he added, such as a stair railing carved like a snake and a fireplace built so that the flames came out of a dragon's mouth. These were not too surprising since Cage has always had unusual tastes. One of his favorite spots in all of Los Angeles, for instance, is the murky La Brea Tar Pits. He says they make him think of the prehistoric monsters that lived there long ago.

Besides fossilized dinosaurs, sea monsters and sea creatures also fascinate Cage. His 1967 Corvette is called the Blue Shark because it has decorations that look like gills. And once, when he had an apartment in Hollywood, he housed several aquariums there. They were filled with sharks and octopuses. In addition, he displayed large exotic bugs in frames on the walls.

Following *It Happened in Paradise,* Nicolas Cage again seemed at a standstill both professionally and personally. But all that was about to change. A low-budget independent film, for which he was paid $240,000 instead of his usual $3 or $4 million, was going to win him an Oscar.

Chapter 4

All Roads Leave from Vegas

L*EAVING LAS VEGAS* (1995) was the breakthrough film for Nicolas Cage, earning him an Academy Award, changing his screen image, and affecting his personal life as well. Cage had seen the movie script while filming *It Happened in Paradise* and knew he had to play the part of a lonely alcoholic who sees no way out of his desperation. Cage says, "Part of my plan has been to constantly change and do the unexpected. I've always believed that these unexpected hidden treasures, like *Leaving Las Vegas*, will keep coming my way. I did it because it was a great role. I did it because it was different."[33]

Cage also said that the making of the movie deeply affected him. He began to think about the kind of characters he was constantly portraying. He began to wonder how his son would be affected by the roles he played. It was this way of thinking that slowly kept pushing his career in a new direction.

The Making of a Winner

Cage so wanted the part in *Leaving Las Vegas* that he agreed to work for far less than he usually received. Cage recalls, "I would never have been able to make *Leaving Las Vegas* if I hadn't had some commercial success before that. If I hadn't had some semblance of a career I never would have had enough money to do that film."[34]

If Cage had deliberately chosen a role to earn him an Oscar, he could not have done better than his part in *Leaving Las Vegas*.

Cage plays Ben, an alcoholic screenwriter who makes no apologies for his drinking. A lonely man, he has lost his family and his career. He takes a room in a run-down motel in Las Vegas with the idea of drinking himself to death. Once in Las Vegas, however, Ben is distracted by Sera (played by Elisabeth Shue), a prostitute. Out of desperation and loneliness, these two self-destructive people form a relationship.

Their growing attachment develops into a moving love story. The movie focuses almost entirely on the two downward-spiraling main characters, and it does not end happily. Critics

> **The Oscars**
>
> The high point of Cage's career to date was winning his first Oscar. The Academy Awards, commonly called the Oscars, are given each year to film artists and technicians by the Academy of Motion Picture Arts and Sciences. The Oscar marks the winner as the best in his or her craft. Members of thirteen art and craft branches select up to five nominees for awards in a particular area of speciality, such as acting, directing, editing, or musical score.
>
> The first Academy Awards were presented in 1927–1928 for the picture *Wings*, about the U.S. Army Air Corps during World War I. The first actors to win an Oscar were Emil Jannings and Janet Gaynor. Other awards given by the film industry include those presented by the Cannes Film Festival in France, the Directors Guild of America, and the Sundance Film Festival, which discovers and develops young filmmakers of American independent films.
>
> *Cage proudly displays his Oscar won for the portrayal of Ben in* Leaving Las Vegas.

called the performances by Cage and Shue magnificent. Critic Roger Ebert said of them, "One scene after another finds the right note.... Cage and Shue make these clichés [the drunk and the prostitute] into unforgettable people.... You sense an observant intelligence peering from inside the drunken man, seeing everything, clearly and sadly."[35]

To prepare for the role, Cage studied other successful actors who had portrayed alcoholics on film. He was mainly inspired by Albert Finney's role in *Under the Volcano* (1984). He also watched Ray Milland in *The Lost Weekend* (1945), Jack Lemmon's powerful performance in *Days of Wine and Roses* (1962), and Dudley Moore as a spoiled, tipsy millionaire in *Arthur* (1981).

Cage's drunkenness may have been inspired by Finney, but it was fine-tuned by his own method of immersing himself in a character. He watched hospital patients with alcohol-withdrawal symptoms. Along with director Mike Figgis and Shue, he spent evenings visiting bars in Los Angeles where he talked about addiction with some of the people he met. And for added realism, Cage made a videotape of himself slowly getting drunk on gin. He wanted to hear how he sounded when he had had too much to drink. Then he erased the tape.

A Fine Romance

After Cage felt he had perfected his role as an alcoholic, filming began. The low-budget independent film was shot during twenty-eight intense days. Figgis could not afford to film in Las Vegas itself, so the whole company moved to Laughlin, about an hour away. Money limitations also made it necessary to record the sound live at the location; big-budget movies usually dub the sound in later. After the movie was in the can—meaning it was completed—nervous time began as producer, director, and actors waited for critical and audience reaction to the film.

By now, however, Nicolas Cage had something else on his mind other than his newest movie. Patricia Arquette, his romance of eight years earlier, was back in his life. The two had kept in touch through the years, so Cage knew that Arquette had a son who was about Weston's age. Early in 1995, Cage ran into her again at Canter's, where they had first met. Two months later,

Nicolas Cage and Patricia Arquette finally married in April 1995, eight years after they initially met.

Arquette called Cage and asked if he still wanted to marry her. His somewhat surprised reply was, "Yeah, OK, I'll do it."[36]

After an eight-year separation, thirty-one-year-old Cage and twenty-seven-year-old Arquette were married two weeks later, in April 1995. The low-key, ten-minute ceremony took place on a hill outside of Carmel on the California coast. The bride wore a black vinyl suit, and the wedding cake had purple frosting.

After their wedding, the couple traveled the United States on their honeymoon, stopping to ride the famous Cyclone roller coaster at Coney Island, New York. After the honeymoon, Cage and Arquette settled down to make a home for their two sons. Although Cage kept his Gothic castle, the newlyweds bought a more traditional home in Malibu. Cage described the first few weeks after their return to California as "somewhat like an arranged marriage" because they really did not know each other very well, but he also said that they were "definitely soulmates."[37]

The Scream Machine

Like thousands of other Americans, Nicolas Cage shares a fascination with roller coasters. The Cyclone at Coney Island, New York City, is certainly not the newest, highest, or fastest, but for pure history, it cannot be beat. It is arguably America's most famous scream machine. Built in 1927, it was the highest, fastest, and steepest drop in the nation—down an eighty-six-foot hill. From there, the coaster flew into a fan turn, tearing down and then up into another large hill, then into another fan turn right out over Surf Avenue. The finish was a dash into the station, where the skid brakes grabbed, and the coaster and riders squealed with delight. Flying ace Charles Lindbergh tried the roller coaster and declared that it was greater than flying an airplane at top speed.

In 1969, through neglect and disuse, the ride was condemned. But a "Save the Cyclone" campaign was instituted, and by July 3, 1975, the famed roller coaster had been refurbished. In 1991, on the Cyclone's sixty-fourth birthday, it was dedicated as a national historic landmark.

Cage and Arquette rode the world-famous Cyclone roller coaster at Coney Island, New York, during their honeymoon.

The Big Time

While Cage was settling his personal life, he was also waiting for reports on *Leaving Las Vegas*. By mid-October encouraging words were coming in from screenings in cities such as Boston, New York, and Chicago. *Rolling Stone* magazine named the movie one of its favorite films that year. Critics began writing about Cage almost as though they were stunned that the wild man could give a performance of such sweetness and clarity. Perhaps no one was saying it out loud, but the unspoken words *Academy Award* were just beneath the surface.

This was a fine time for Nicolas Cage. He had married Arquette. His mother seemed to be pulling out of her depressive state; she now lived nearby, and Cage saw her frequently. And when the Academy Award nominations were announced, Cage was up for best actor. The only depressing note was Cage's father, Augie. After seeing *Leaving Las Vegas*, he had commented on his son's career and used the word *epitaph*. Presumably, he used the word to mean a crowning achievement, but the press reported the remark as though Augie meant the movie would kill his son's career. In any case, Augie was upset when his remark made the headlines. Despite the fact that the dispute was between Augie and the press, father and son quarreled once again.

Cage's argument with his father was overshadowed by his invitation to attend the sixty-eighth annual Academy Awards held on March 25, 1996. The lavish presentation of the awards each March had become a mega television affair, reaching some 1 billion viewers worldwide. The Academy Awards still carry great weight for the film industry's economics since an Oscar for best picture can put tens of millions of added dollars in the studio's bank account. A best actor award, for which Cage was nominated, practically ensures that the star can write his or her own salary ticket on the next job.

The Coppola family, without Augie, attended the Awards ceremony that night. If Cage won, he would be the third member of his family to earn an Oscar, joining the ranks of his uncle Francis and his grandfather Carmine, who won for his musical score of *The Godfather Part 2*. Near the end of a long evening, the Best Actor Award was announced. Jessica Lange presented the Oscar, and Cage later said that all he heard was her saying the letter *N*.

The offbeat, unpredictable actor had finally made the big time. To do so, he had to beat out his longtime friend Sean Penn, who played a condemned prisoner in *Dead Man Walking*, one-time Oscar winner Sir Anthony Hopkins as the brilliant but psychotic Hannibal Lecter in *Silence of the Lambs*; one-time winner Richard Dreyfuss in *Mr. Holland's Opus*; and Italian star Massimo Troisi in *Il Postino*. Cage said of his Oscar-winning performance, "I never expected people to see the film and I certainly didn't expect to win any awards from it.... I did it because it was a great role. The amazing thing is that... for the first time in my life my tastes were in synch with other people's. How weird is that?"[38]

For Cage, it must have seemed as though the past fifteen years of ups and downs in his career had finally paid off. He said he felt as though the Oscar was recognition that he had not really been so crazy in his choice of roles all those years. He was further honored that September with the Lifetime Achievement Award at the Montreal World Film Festival, the youngest honoree in the award's history.

It was noted at the Montreal festival that Cage accepted the award wearing a somber dark suit and tie. That attire might have been a reaction to *People* magazine's award a few months earlier naming Cage as Hollywood's "worst dressed." In the *People* article, costume designer Bob Ringwood said Cage dressed like "a band leader off duty," and another observed that Cage "has his own personal style—and it's bad."[39] Comments such as these tend to irritate Cage to a great degree, even though he seems to have listened to the critics.

The Action Hero

Now that the Academy Award had established his new image, Cage took his career in a new direction. He switched to a popular genre of the late twentieth and early twenty-first centuries: the action hero. But even there, he added his own distinctive flavor to the role. Not interested in the James Bond type who operates as a superhero without limitations or flaws, Cage wanted to portray the action hero as a vulnerable being who is simply trying his best to succeed.

In Cage's first venture into the action-hero genre, he costarred with movie legend Sean Connery in *The Rock* (1996). Connery portrays British secret agent John Mason, the only man ever to break out of "the Rock," the nickname of the now-

All Roads Leave from Vegas

Oscar award-winners Cage and Susan Sarandon share a joyful moment at the 1996 Academy Awards.

unoccupied Alcatraz prison in San Francisco Bay, California. The Rock is an island comprising twenty-two acres of forbidding stone. From 1934 to 1963, it was the most feared prison in the United States, at least in the public perception. Despite the plot of *The Rock*, officially no prisoner ever escaped from Alcatraz.

In this movie, Connery is teamed with Cage, an FBI chemical weapons expert named Stanley Goodspeed. They must stop a disgruntled U.S. Marine Corps general (Ed Harris) who takes over the prison from wiping out San Francisco with poison gas. Much of Cage's own personality comes through in this film, and he claims to have rewritten much of his dialogue. Since director Michael Bay allowed him a good deal of leeway, Cage was even permitted to change his character's name from Bill to Stanley because he felt the new name portrayed the character more honestly.

The Rock, which was actually filmed on Alcatraz, was a winner with audiences. Fans liked the duo of Connery and Cage. The film grossed $134 million in the United States and an unheard-of $335 million worldwide. It is Cage's biggest commercial hit so far, topping *Moonstruck*. Although it was a hit with fans, *The Rock* received mixed reviews from the critics. *USA Today* thought the movie was funny because it did not regard itself as anything more than junk. Roger Ebert liked the two stars, saying, "What really works is the chemistry between Connery and Cage. It's interesting to see how good actors...can find a way to occupy the center of this whirlwind with characters who somehow manage to be quirky and convincing."[40]

Cage's response to audience reaction was to try another action role in *Con Air* (1997). This action hero was to Cage's liking because it did not follow the usual trend of a character with almost limitless powers, such as Connery playing James Bond or Sylvester Stallone as Rambo. In *Con Air*, the hero is a nice, fallible guy. Cage is Cameron Poe, a military ranger who eight years earlier was sentenced to jail for an accidental killing. Now he is

Sean Connery (left) stars with Nicolas Cage in Cage's first action movie, The Rock, *which was filmed on Alcatraz.*

going home to his wife on a U.S. Marshal flight that is also carrying several high-security prisoners. Once in flight, the prisoners take over. When Poe is given a chance to get off the plane at its first landing, he refuses because he does not want to abandon the other passengers who are in danger. Instead, he pretends to be on the side of the hijackers. The action culminates with a crash landing and an incredible high-speed chase on the Las Vegas strip.

Again, the audiences loved Cage, and the critics by and large did not. But he defends his entry into the blockbuster, blow-everything-up route: "I have always wanted to make action movies. As a kid, I was drawn to fast cars and [daredevil] Evel Knievel and motorcycles. I still am. It's a sincere expression on some level, on some part of my personality."[41]

Cage Teams with Travolta

His next action movie, *Face/Off* (1997), paired him with another top Hollywood star also known for his fascination with cars and odd films, John Travolta. Directed by John Woo, noted for his powerful staging of action scenes, the movie centers on arch-terrorist Castor Troy (Cage). FBI agent Sean Archer (Travolta) has been after him for years, partly because Troy is the mastermind of terror and destruction and partly because he killed Archer's young son. Early in the film, Troy is captured and falls into a coma. However, he has left a time bomb somewhere in Los Angeles, which will destroy most of the city. To discover the bomb's whereabouts, Archer agrees to assume Troy's identity—literally by altering his own face through an operation—and then go into a maximum-security prison to trick Troy's psychotic brother into revealing where the bomb is hidden.

Odd as the premise sounds, Cage and Travolta obviously had fun with this movie, and the critics liked it, too. As the *San Francisco Chronicle* notes, "Travolta and Cage do more than switch roles. They switch styles. Travolta adopts Cage's abrupt gestures, crazy laugh and tilt of the head, while Cage amazingly embodies Travolta's soulfulness (as well as his tendency to stammer in emotional moments)."[42] *Esquire* magazine comments, "Stars John Travolta and Nicolas Cage and director John Woo

John Travolta (left) pairs up with Cage in the action movie Face/Off.

are all at the top of their game in *Face/Off,* and action-movie gamesmanship doesn't get much better than that."[43]

After making a romantic film called *City of Angels* (1998) with Meg Ryan, Cage returned to the action-hero genre with the thriller *Snake Eyes* (1998), directed by the brash master of suspense Brian De Palma. Here, Cage plays a corrupt cop in Atlantic City, New Jersey, who is trying to solve a murder that occurred during a heavyweight championship boxing match. The movie received lukewarm reviews from both critics and audiences.

While filming *Snake Eyes,* Cage lost a title role in another movie. He was considered for the upcoming mega film *Superman.* Delays in the shooting of *Snake Eyes* caused an overlap in the scheduling of the two movies, and the *Superman* producers, counting on a fantastic hit at the box office, would not delay shooting. To most of his fans, Cage seemed like a highly improbable Superman anyway. He may have passed for Clark Kent, but it was hard to imagine the now balding actor suddenly sporting tights and portraying the strongest man on Earth.

A Not-So-Fine Romance

Although he was passed up for the Superman role in 1999, Cage's career was on solid footing. He was now appearing in more conventional roles, and his fan base was growing. He was feeling more sure of himself and felt he could leave some of the odd antics behind and tackle other areas.

His career was doing well, but his marriage was in trouble. About nine months after the wedding, Cage and Arquette separated. She moved to Studio City, and Cage divided his time among his homes in Bel Air, Malibu, and the castle in the Hollywood Hills.

During this unstable time, Cage made one movie with his actress wife, *Bringing Out the Dead* (1999). Cage plays Frank, a burned-out paramedic in the West Side section of New York City known as Hell's Kitchen. He is slowly going crazy from all the death and violence he sees in his everyday job, and he is especially haunted by the memory of a young girl whose life he could not save. Then, Frank meets Mary (Arquette), a recovering drug addict, and the two try to redeem their lives together. Although it did poorly at the box office, one reviewer said it had "dark humor, amusing moments" and "[Cage] gives a blazing, implosive performance."[44]

During the filming of *Bringing Out the Dead*, Cage and Arquette appeared to be on good terms with each other. Coworkers remarked that they were always friendly and seemed at ease on and off the set. However, in an interview following the movie, Arquette was asked how they could work together under the circumstances. She replied that to keep things calm and on a professional level, "we went to work in separate cars and had separate trailers on the set."[45]

Feeling Good About Cage

As a new century began, Nicolas Cage may not have found the key to personal happiness and success, but as an actor, he looked as if he was well on his way. He said that after winning the Oscar, he tried to achieve some emotional balance in both his professional and personal lives. He began looking after himself more, cutting down on drinking and giving up smoking. His fits of anger occurred less frequently and were more controlled. He blamed some of his temper outbursts on coffee. "I cut all the coffee out of my diet," he said, "so I don't get anxiety attacks

By the year 2000, Cage had made several lifestyle adjustments in an attempt to achieve a better emotional balance.

anymore. I have to be in a good place and what I mean by good isn't necessarily happy but where I'm functioning, where I know that I feel well." He admitted to a new feeling of financial responsibility about himself, which he tries to instill in his son. "I try to teach the value of the dollar," he said, explaining that he breaks down Weston's allowance in three ways: "One-third you're going to save, one-third you're going to spend on what you want and the last third you're going to give to charity."[46]

Nicolas Cage may not have reached his desired level of emotional balance as the year 2000 rang in, but he was a long way from the actor who threw chairs on the set when he could not have his way. Now he was bent on expanding his skills and developing a richness of character and depth that his fans had not yet experienced. He knew he could never leave the old Cage behind entirely, yet he also knew his talent could make him one of a handful of seriously great actors on the silver screen.

Chapter 5

The Professional Nonconformist

A TALENTED AND dedicated actor at the top of his craft, Nicolas Cage remains to some extent what he has always been—a professional nonconformist. Although he acknowledges that he will never quite fit the mold of disciplined leading man, he wants to be recognized professionally as a serious actor who approaches each new part with thoroughness and passion. He has gained the confidence to try new roles and new directions in his career.

But before he could continue in a new direction, he felt he needed to end his marriage to Patricia Arquette. As unsettled as the marriage had been, so went the divorce. In early 2000, Cage filed divorce papers citing differences that could not be reconciled. Yet a few weeks later, the divorce papers were withdrawn, and Arquette said they were reunited to celebrate their sixth anniversary. The differences remained, however, for the final divorce was granted on August 29, 2001. Cage has had very little to say about the breakup of his first marriage.

Vampires and Romance

While facing the end of his marriage in 2000, Cage went back to an old interest in his career—vampires. But this time he was behind the camera rather than in front of it. The film *Shadow of the Vampire* (2000) was Cage's first venture into producing. This is a colorful and amusing story about the making of the classically creepy, grandfather-of-all-vampire-movies, *Nosferatu* (1922).

John Malkovich plays director F. W. Murnau, who travels to Czechoslovakia to re-create the story of Bram Stoker's *Dracula*. Since he wants to create a more realistic vampire film, Murnau recruits a real vampire, whose payment is the leading lady, Greta, after the movie is finished. As the shooting of the film progresses, the vampire tries to keep his end of the bargain, for instance, only appearing on the set in the dark of night. However, he cannot resist his bloodthirsty ways, and the cast begins to disappear, one by one. Critics called it highly imaginative fiction, and audiences liked it, too.

Cage's first experience as a producer went well overall, and he seemed to enjoy this new role. "John [Malkovich] and Willem [Dafoe] had never worked together before," he said. "The film allowed me to team up two of my favorite actors and put them into the hands of a pure artist [director E. Elias Merhige]. I'd seen Elias' first feature, *Begotten*, and found it completely compelling. When I read the script, I saw it as the perfect vehicle for

Modeled upon the making of the 1922 vampire film Nosferatu, *Cage's first experience as a producer came with* Shadow of the Vampire *in 2000. Willem Dafoe (pictured) appeared in Cage's film.*

his talents."[47] Cage set up his production company, Saturn Films, in 1996. He is constantly looking for good scripts for his company to produce.

Cage was back in front of the camera for *Gone in Sixty Seconds* (2000), a movie he chose based on his fascination with high-class cars. He plays reformed criminal Randall "Memphis" Raines, who is called on to do what he used to do best—steal cars—to save his brother's life. His brother had promised a local crime lord that he would deliver fifty high-class cars within a specified time period. However, that becomes impossible when the police uncover his chop shop, an illegal operation where stolen cars are repainted or their parts are switched to other vehicles. Without the cars, the brother will be killed. So, Memphis has one night to steal fifty cars; the film's title comes from the fact that sixty seconds is about how long it takes this master car thief to unlock a car and speed away. Critics and audiences were not so kind to this one.

Cage did far better with almost all the critics in his third movie of 2000, *The Family Man*, a romantic comedy. He plays a wealthy and ruthless Wall Street executive named Jack Campbell whose life is completely changed one Christmas Eve. When he meets a stranger who asks whether he is missing anything in life, Campbell says no, and the stranger gives him a mysterious warning. The next morning Campbell wakes up in a suburban New Jersey home and discovers he is married to his high school sweetheart. Critics called it smart and sentimental and praised Cage's performance. Said one reviewer, "Cage is not only credible but he is perfect as the confused protagonist who is knocked down from his perch of wealth and power and left to wander through the mediocrity of suburbia without a map."[48]

Cage was not only busy on the screen as the new century began, but he was feeling comfortable about himself in whatever role he chose. He was gaining new respect in Hollywood, and with that status came a new freedom.

For his first film of 2001, Cage played in a period-piece romance called *Captain Corelli's Mandolin*. Set on the Greek island of Cephallonia during World War II, the movie tells of the growing romance between Italian army commander Corelli and the

Corelli's Passion

Captain Corelli, as played by Nicolas Cage, has a great passion in his life—the mandolin. Cage himself does not count musical instruments as one of his passions, but he says he worked very hard to learn to play the mandolin well enough to satisfy audiences and some critics. The mandolin evolved during the eighteenth century and is related to the lute, a stringed instrument with a pear-shaped body and a long neck. It was built in several varieties in many Italian towns, with the Neapolitan mandolin becoming the most representative. Pasquale Vinaccia of Naples (1806–1882) strongly influenced the look of the mandolin as we know it today. It has four pairs of steel strings with a pear-shaped body and fingerboard. During the twentieth century, the mandolin was built in a range of sizes, from soprano to contrabass. A shallow, flat-backed version of the mandolin is most likely to be seen in the United States as a part of bluegrass string bands.

For his role in Captain Corelli's Mandolin, *Cage learned how to play the small stringed instrument.*

beautiful Pelagia (played by Penelope Cruz), who is engaged to a local fisherman. The scenery is breathtaking and audiences enjoyed the love story, but critics generally found the film lacking in depth. Some critics, however, praised Cage's performance: "I found Cage completely endearing as the musical Italian captain.... Although Cage's Italian accent is somewhat off-putting at first, he settles into the role of a soldier trapped in a war he doesn't believe in with conviction and sensitivity. I loved watching him play the mandolin. He seemed to feel the music in his soul."[49] Cage later said he had no musical ability and no training, but his approach to the mandolin was constant practice.

The Second Time Around

Whereas Cage's career was busy and productive, his private life remained pretty much that—private. Reportedly, during the filming of *Captain Corelli's Mandolin* in late 2000, he had been seen around town with his costar Cruz. Then, in October, he went to a birthday party given for guitarist Johnny Ramone. At the party was Lisa Marie Presley, the only child of the late Elvis. Cage and Presley got into a conversation that night, initiated by Cage's admission of his longtime interest in—and sometime imitation of—her father. The two learned that they also shared a fascination with old cars.

The party was not the last time they saw each other. In May 2001 thirty-eight-year-old Cage and thirty-four-year-old Presley were seen together at a Tom Jones concert in Las Vegas. In July they attended a Washington, D.C., ceremony honoring the Navajo people, the subject of Cage's movie *Windtalkers*. Later in the month Cage went with Presley to Memphis, where she cut the ribbon to signify the opening of an apartment building for homeless families, a project of her charitable foundation.

Then, shortly before sunset on August 10, 2002, Cage and Presley were married at a small ceremony in Hawaii. Before the ceremony, at Presley's request, they had tried to contact her deceased father during a séance. It was not reported whether they thought the contact was successful. This was the third marriage for Presley, whose first marriage to musician Danny Keough resulted in two children, Danielle and Benjamin.

The wedding, which occurred just a few days before the twenty-fifth anniversary of Elvis Presley's death, was attended by Lisa Marie's mother, Priscilla Presley. Thirteen-year-old Danielle was the flower girl, and Weston Cage, twelve years old, and Benjamin, ten, were ring bearers. Newspaper reporters jokingly asked Cage if he wore blue suede shoes to the wedding, a reference to the popular song by Elvis.

Both Cage and Presley share custody of their children. The extended family spent time at Cage's Bel Air home and Presley's in Los Angeles.

The couple remained in the news with reports that Cage had begun to practice Buddhism. Later, it was said both Presley and

Lisa Marie Presley Cage

Lisa Marie Presley, whom Cage married in August 2002, has been in the national spotlight practically all of her life. She is the only child of Elvis and Priscilla Presley, so she was never far from somebody's camera and criticism. Like Cage, she has been cited for dressing badly. She even made Mr. Blackwell's Worst Dressed List for 1988. Blackwell has made a career of his annual list, in which he sarcastically describes the apparel of many stars. However, some say the publicity is worth the sarcasm.

Although Lisa Marie has had problems, such as experimenting with drugs as a youth, she has overcome them and is now better known for her charitable works. She spends a good deal of her time at charitable functions and also at events that honor Elvis. In August 2002, for instance, she appeared in Memphis, Tennessee, at the twenty-fifth anniversary concert in his memory.

Like countless celebrities, Nicolas Cage and Lisa Marie Presley experienced a short-term romance—they married in August 2002 and were divorced by November of the same year.

Cage were following Scientology, a religious movement begun by L. Ron Hubbard. But fans were most startled when it was announced in late November 2002 that Cage had filed for divorce citing irreconcilable differences. When interviewed, Presley said they never should have married. Cage had no comment.

Back to the Wars

Cage had begun the year 2002 with a new movie. For this World War II film, he starred as U.S. Marine sergeant Joe Enders in *Windtalkers*. Directed by John Woo, with whom Cage worked in *Face/Off*, it is the story of two marines who must shield a pair of Navajo codetalkers from the Japanese at all costs during the Battle of Saipan. The two Navajos, called windtalkers, or codetalkers, are being trained to transmit information because their native language can be turned into a code that cannot be easily translated by the Japanese. Cage's character does not want to get too close to the Navajo men. He knows he might have to kill them to prevent their capture.

Navajo codetalkers work amidst a battle against the Japanese in the 1940s. Cage starred in the film of their story, portraying a U.S. Marine sergeant who must protect such windtalkers during World War II.

The People of *Windtalkers*

In June 2002 a ceremony was held in Washington, D.C., in which the Congressional Medal of Honor was presented to the four surviving members of the original Navajo codetalkers. Cage was only one of a handful of Hollywood showbusiness personalities invited to attend this ceremony due to his affiliation with the movie *Windtalkers* and his interest in the Navajo people. Cage expressed his deep admiration for the Navajo during the filming. *Windtalkers* centers around the language of the Navajo (also spelled Navaho). The most populous of all Native American groups in the United States, there are some one hundred thousand Navajo living in Arizona, northwestern New Mexico, and southeastern Utah.

The movie focuses on their language, which, as the U.S. military found during World War II, is almost impossible to decode. Navajo is a tone language, meaning that the tone or pitch of the voice helps to distinguish the words. Merely by changing the tone of his or her voice, a Navajo speaker may change the meaning of a word. There is a separate grammatical category that allows a speaker to talk to someone who is present in a crowd without naming the person. Names are believed to have various powers, so it is considered impolite to speak another's name aloud in company. Adding to the difficulty of understanding the language, verb forms change meaning according to shape. For instance, the verb form for holding a stick is different from the verb form for holding a ball. These intricate and unique language differences make Navajo speech virtually impossible for an outsider to understand or decipher.

Generally, critics did not show much enthusiasm over Cage's performance in *Windtalkers*. *New York Times* critic Elvis Mitchell comments that "Mr. Cage's presence is such that we still want more from him."[50] Cage's fans were generally lukewarm toward the film.

The Fan Base

Every successful actor has a solid base of loyal fans, and Cage is no exception. They have followed him through vampires and cockroach eating, through bad films and good ones, through dreadful reviews and an Academy Award. In turn, Nicolas Cage has always been an actor who has appreciated the people who go to see him on the screen. In public and in interviews, he acknowledges how important his audience is to him and his career.

Unlike many Hollywood and stage pesonalities, Cage remains a most approachable star. In contrast to the often strange,

The Professional Nonconformist

withdrawn characters he has portrayed, he is very down-to-earth with his fans. He is a bona fide member of the "rich and famous" and he lives like one, but with his fans at least he does not act like one. It is not unusual for him to leave a restaurant, for example, and dart across the street to shake hands with an ardent fan who calls his name. That willingness to chat with fans and his obvious talent make Nicolas Cage a great hit with the audiences that have been so loyal to him.

After winning the Oscar, Cage also talked about the reaction of fans on a personal level. He said of the day after the awards ceremony,

> The next morning I'm downtown, and I'm walking by the newsstand, and it was the first time I'd ever been on the front page of the newspaper, which was...interesting. Then I went to this old coffee shop to have a cup of coffee and some pancakes, and the cooks and chefs come out and clap, and it was a great feeling. Then I get in my car and put my Beatles song on that I play when

Cage poses with a fan. He reportedly enjoys meeting his supporters in public.

I'm feeling proud, which is "Baby You're a Rich Man." So I'm listening to that in my Lamborghini and I'm driving to the beach, feeling pretty good, when a cop pulls me over. And I think I'm going to get a ticket, which is what normally happens in that car, but they say, "We just want to say congratulations." And that was cool. And I'm walking on the beach and surfers from, like hundreds of yards in are going, "Hey, Nick, congratulations!" And it was just a wild day. For one second, Los Angeles felt like a small town.[51]

The Nonconformist

Cage seems confident about his career, but even he is not sure where a new idea will lead him. He certainly will continue to act, but he will produce movies and perhaps direct them as well. According to Cage,

> I never want to lose the ability to just go for it. The one thing I had hoped the Oscar would give me more than anything else was that if I came up with an idea that seemed a little left field, you'd just give me five more seconds before you kill it.... Because sometimes they [the ideas] can work. And I still don't get that. I get maybe two and half seconds. I don't get the five seconds I was hoping for.[52]

Talented, unpredictable Nicolas Cage has emerged through the good and the bad, the criticized and the acclaimed as one of Hollywood's top actors and leading men. It is obvious that no matter where his career leads, he will continue to be himself. On screen and off, Cage is a man who always follows his heart, always searches for depth in his characters, and is always ready to question and improvise. Perhaps down the road, he may even get the five seconds he is looking for.

Notes

Introduction: Instead of Jail
1. Quoted in Douglas Thompson, *Uncaged*. London: Boxtree, 1997, p. 8.
2. Quoted in Brian J. Robb, *Nicolas Cage: Hollywood's Wild Talent*. London: Plexus, 1998, p. 6.

Chapter 1: Destined for the Screen
3. Quoted in Thompson, *Uncaged*, p. 26.
4. Quoted in Robb, *Nicolas Cage*, p. 11.
5. Quoted in Thompson, *Uncaged*, p. 30.
6. Quoted in Robb, *Nicolas Cage*, p. 17.
7. Quoted in Thompson, *Uncaged*, p. 19.
8. Quoted in Leonard Maltin, *2000 Movie and Video Guide*. New York: Signet, 1999, p. 1185.

Chapter 2: Odd Man Out
9. Mark Rowland, "The Beasts Within...Nicolas Cage," *American Film*, June 1990, p. 24.
10. Quoted in Maltin, *2000 Movie and Video Guide*, p. 493.
11. Quoted in Robb, *Nicolas Cage*, p. 26.
12. Quoted in Fred Schruers, "Nicolas Cage Is a Hollywood Samurai," *Rolling Stone*, November 16, 1995, p. 93.
13. Quoted in Thompson, *Uncaged*, p. 71.
14. Quoted in Robb, *Nicolas Cage*, p. 45.

15. Quoted in Maltin, *2000 Movie and Video Guide*, p. 1061.
16. Quoted in *Current Biography*, "Nicolas Cage." New York: Wilson, 1983, p. 4.
17. Quoted in Robb, *Nicolas Cage*, p. 52.
18. Peter Reiher, "Raising Arizona." http://fmg-www.cs.ucla.edu.
19. Quoted in *Current Biography*, "Nicolas Cage," p. 4.

Chapter 3: Toward a New Image

20. Quoted in Robb, *Nicolas Cage*, p. 57.
21. Quoted in Roger Ebert, "Moonstruck." www.suntimes.com.
22. Quoted in Thompson, *Uncaged*, p. 94.
23. Quoted in Thompson, *Uncaged*, p. 100.
24. Quoted in Lily Chin, "The Cage File," *Pittsburgh Post-Gazette*, June 9, 2000, p. 20.
25. Quoted in Maltin, *2000 Movie and Video Guide*, p. 1495.
26. Quoted in Lucy Kaylin, "The Rebel at Rest," *GQ*, March 1997, p. 224.
27. Quoted in Robb, *Nicolas Cage*, p. 81.
28. Quoted in Maltin, *2000 Movie and Video Guide*, p. 149.
29. Quoted in Robb, *Nicolas Cage*, p. 83.
30. Ellen Hawkes, "Now I Recognize That Consequences Matter," *Parade*, June 9, 2002, p. 4.
31. James Berardinelli, "Guarding Tess." http://moviereviews.colossus.net.
32. Maltin, *2000 Movie and Video Guide*, p. 87.

Chapter 4: All Roads Leave from Vegas

33. Quoted in Robb, *Nicolas Cage*, p. 106–7.
34. Quoted in Robb, *Nicolas Cage*, p. 106–7.
35. Roger Ebert, "Leaving Las Vegas." www.suntimes.com.
36. Quoted in Robb, *Nicolas Cage*, p. 118.
37. Quoted in Beth Ursin, "Biography of Nicolas Cage." http://members.aol.com/eursin/bio.htm.

38. Quoted in Thompson, *Uncaged*, p. 15.
39. Quoted in Robb, *Nicolas Cage*, p. 121.
40. Quoted in Roger Ebert, "The Rock," *Chicago Sun-Times*, September 1996.
41. Quoted in Fred Schruers, "The Passion of Nicolas Cage," November 11, 1999, p. 94.
42. Quoted in Robb, *Nicolas Cage*, p. 145.
43. Quoted in Rotten Tomatoes, "Face/Off (1997)." http://www.rottentomatoes.com.
44. Quoted in VCD Gallery, "Bringing Out the Dead (1999)." www.vcdgallery.com.
45. Quoted in *People Weekly*, "No More Acting," March 13, 2000, p. 84.
46. Quoted in Schruers, "The Passion of Nicolas Cage" p. 94.

Chapter 5: The Professional Nonconformist
47. Quoted in Elizabeth Lawrence, "Movie Review," 2001. www.theromanceclub.com.
48. Quoted in "The Family Man Movie Review," 2000. www.preview-online.com.
49. Quoted in Anthony Leong, "*Captain Corelli's Mandolin* Movie Review," 2000. www.mediacircus.net.
50. Quoted in Elvis Mitchell, "Of Duty, Friendship, and a Navajo Dilemma," *New York Times*, June 14, 2002, p. E14.
51. Quoted in Kaylin, "The Rebel at Rest," p. 224.
52. Quoted in Kaylin, "The Rebel at Rest," p. 224.

Important Dates in the Life of Nicolas Cage

1964
Nicolas Kim Coppola is born on January 7.

1976
His parents divorce; he moves with his father to Beverly Hills, California.

1979–1980
Takes drama lessons in high school; passes the General Educational Development test; leaves school in senior year.

1982
Gets minor part in *Fast Times at Ridgemont High.*

1983
Has part in *The Outsiders*; changes name to Nicolas Cage; appears in his uncle's production of *Rumble Fish.*

1984
Lands first starring role as Nicky in *Racing with the Moon* with Sean Penn; appears in *The Cotton Club* as Vincent "Mad Dog" Dwyer; trashes trailer in temper tantrum; appears as Al in *Birdy.*

1986
Plays Ned Hanlan in *The Boy in Blue*; stars as Charlie in *Peggy Sue Got Married.*

1987
Appears as H. I. McConnough in *Raising Arizona*, his ninth film; presents leading-man image as Ronny in *Moonstruck*; meets future wife Patricia Arquette.

1988
Has nonspeaking role in *Never on Tuesday*.

1989
Stars as Peter Lowe in *Vampire's Kiss* and eats a live cockroach.

1992
Plays Michael Williams in *Red Rock West*.

1993
Appears in *Amos and Andrew* and *Deadfall*.

1994
Plays Bill Firpo in *It Happened in Paradise*; portrays Little Junior Brown in *Kiss of Death*.

1995
Appears as Ben in *Leaving Las Vegas*; marries Arquette in April.

1996
Receives Academy Award as best actor for *Leaving Las Vegas* on April 25; stars with Sean Connery in *The Rock* as Stanley Goodspeed.

1997
Appears as Cameron Poe in action movie *Con Air* and as Castor Troy in *Face/Off* with John Travolta.

1998
Stars in *City of Angels* as the angel Seth with Meg Ryan; his part in *Snake Eyes* causes him to miss starring in *Superman*.

1999
Has a role in *8MM*; stars with Arquette in *Bringing Out the Dead*.

2000
Produces *Shadow of the Vampire*; stars in *Gone in Sixty Seconds* and *The Family Man*; meets Lisa Marie Presley.

2001
Divorces Arquette on August 29; appears in *Captain Corelli's Mandolin*.

2002
Appears as Joe Enders in *Windtalkers*; marries Presley in Hawaii on August 10; files for divorce in November.

For Further Reading

Books

Malcolm S. Forbes, *What Happened to Their Kids? Children of the Rich and Famous.* New York: Simon & Schuster, 1990. This book tells about the families of the stars.

Kathrine Krohn, *Elvis Presley the King.* Minneapolis: Lerner, 1993. A look back at the superstar entertainer.

Caral Marling, *Graceland.* Cambridge, MA: Harvard University Press, 1996. A tour through one of the most visited sites in the United States.

Michael Schumacher, *Francis Ford Coppola: A Filmmaker's Life.* New York: Crown, 2001. A biography of the famed director.

Periodicals

In Style, "Nick's Night," February 2002.

People Weekly, "Nicolas Cage and Lisa Marie Presley Wed in Hawaii," August 26, 2002.

Variety, "Gilded Cage," November 5, 12, 2001.

Works Consulted

Books

Current Biography, "Nicolas Cage." New York: Wilson, 1983. An encyclopedic reference including Cage's career accomplishments.

Leonard Maltin, *2000 Movie and Video Guide*. New York: Signet, 1999. This comprehensive, best-selling movie guide is updated annually.

Brian J. Robb, *Nicolas Cage: Hollywood's Wild Talent*. London: Plexus, 1998. A biography of the actor focusing on his personality and its effect on his career.

Douglas Thomson, *Uncaged*. London: Boxtree, 1997. A biography with emphasis on Cage's personal life.

Periodicals

Frank Bruni, "In the Name of the Father," *New York Times Magazine*, May 19, 2002.

Lily Chin, "The Cage File," *Pittsburgh Post-Gazette*, June 9, 2000.

Joe Connelly, "My Life as Nic Cage," *Esquire*, November 1999.

Roger Ebert, "*The Rock*," *Chicago Sun-Times*, September 1996.

Ellen Hawkes, "Now I Recognize That Consequences Matter," *Parade*, June 9, 2002.

Michael Johnsen, "The Godfather of Film: Coppola Rumbles Hollywood," *Video Age International*, February 2000.

Lucy Kaylin, "The Rebel at Rest," *GQ*, March 1997.

Elvis Mitchell, "Of Duty, Friendship, and a Navajo Dilemma," *New York Times,* June 14, 2002.

People Weekly, "No More Acting," March 13, 2000.

Mark Rowland, "The Beasts Within... Nicolas Cage," *American Film,* June 1990.

Karen S. Schneider, "Love Thee Tender," *People Weekly,* October 8, 2001.

Fred Schruers, "Nicolas Cage Is a Hollywood Samurai," *Rolling Stone,* November 16, 1995.

———, "The Passion of Nicolas Cage," *Rolling Stone,* November 11, 1999.

Kate Sheehy, "Lisa Marie Weds Nicolas Cage," *New York Post,* August 13, 2002.

Internet Sources

All-Reviews.com "*City of Angels.*" www.all-reviews.com.

Apollo Movie Guide, "*Honeymoon in Vegas.*" http://apolloguide.com.

James Berardinelli, "*Guarding Tess.*" http://moviereviews.colossus.net.

Roger Ebert, "*Leaving Las Vegas.*" www.suntimes.com.

"*Family Man* Movie Review," 2000. www.preview-online.com.

Hollywood.com, "*Shadow of the Vampire.*" www.hollywood.com.

Internet Movie Database, "*Sonny* (2002)." http://us.imdb.com.

Elizabeth Lawrence, "*Leaving Las Vegas.*" http://moviereviews.colossus.net.

———, "Movie Review," 2001. www.theromanceclub.com.

Anthony Leong, "*Captain Corelli's Mandolin* Movie Review," 2000. www.mediacircus.net.

———, "*Moonstruck.*" www.suntimes.com.

Peter Reiher, "*Raising Arizona.*" http://fmg-www.cs.ucla.edu.

Rotten Tomatoes, "*Face/Off* (1997)." www.rottentomatoes.com.

Works Consulted

Beth Ursin, "Biography of Nicolas Cage." http://members.aol.com/eursin/bio.htm.

U.S. Department of Justice, Federal Bureau of Prisons, "A Brief History of Alcatraz." www.bop.gov.

VCD Gallery, "*Bringing Out the Dead.*" www.vcdgallery.com.

Yahoo! Movies, "*Captain Corelli's Mandolin* (2001)." http://movies.yahoo.com.

Index

Academy Award, 6, 56, 57, 61–62
action films, 62–66
American Graffiti (film), 13
Amos and Andrew (film), 52
Apocalypse Now (film), 27
Arquette, Patricia, 44–45, 58–59, 67, 69

Berardinelli, James, 52
Bergman, Andrew, 53
Best of Times, The (television show), 20
Beverly Hills High, 13
Birdy (film), 33
Boy in Blue, The (film), 33
Brando, Marlon, 31–32
Brat Pack, 30–33
Bringing Out the Dead (film), 67

Cage, Nicolas
   acting ability of, 6–7, 25, 52–53
   action films by, 62–66
   in *Bringing Out the Dead*, 67
   in *Captain Corelli's Mandolin*, 71–72
   childhood of, 9–15
   in comedic roles, 50–53
   in *Con Air*, 64–65
   in *The Cotton Club*, 27–30
   early acting career of, 19–24
   in *Face/Off*, 65–66
   in *The Family Man*, 71
   family of, 6, 8–14, 16, 27–28
   fans of, 76–78
   fatherhood for, 48, 50, 68
   in *Fire Birds*, 47
   future for, 78
   in *Gone in Sixty Seconds*, 71
   in *Guarding Tess*, 52
   in high school, 13–15
   in *Honeymoon in Vegas*, 50–52
   imagination of, 10–11
   interest in acting of, 10–12, 16–19
   in *It Could Happen to You*, 53, 54
   in *It Happened in Paradise*, 53–54
   in *Leaving Las Vegas*, 56–58, 60–62

lifestyle adjustments for, 67–68
in *Moonstruck*, 40–42
name change by, 21–23
Oscar won by, 6, 56, 57, 61–62
in *Peggy Sue Got Married*, 34–36
personal life of, 36, 44–46, 50, 54–55, 58–59, 73–75
as producer, 69–71
in *Racing with the Moon*, 27
in *Raising Arizona*, 36–39
reaches celebrity status, 43–44
relationship with father of, 16–17, 19, 27, 61
relationship with Lisa Marie Presley, 73–75
relationship with Patricia Arquette, 44–45, 58–59, 67, 69
in *The Rock*, 62–64
in *Snake Eyes*, 66
study of acting by, 17–19
temper of, 15, 30, 42, 44, 67–68
unconventional personality of, 6–7
unusual tastes of, 54–55, 62
in *Valley Girl*, 25–27
in *Vampire's Kiss*, 46
in *Wild at Heart*, 48–49
wild behavior of, 48–50
in *Windtalkers*, 75–76
Cage, Weston Coppola (son), 48
Captain Corelli's Mandolin (film), 71–72
Cher, 40–42
childhood, 9–15
City of Angels (film), 66
Coen brothers, 36–39
Con Air (film), 64–65
Connery, Sean, 62–63
Conversation, The (film), 14
Coppola, August "Augie" (father), 9–10
divorce of, 12–13
frustration felt by, 15
relationship with Cage, 19, 27, 61
view of acting profession by, 16–17, 19
Coppola, Carmine (grandfather), 8
Coppola, Francis Ford (uncle)
career of, 6, 28
celebrity of, 8–9, 13–14, 16, 27
films with Cage and, 21, 23, 34, 35
Coppola, Joy Vogelsang (mother), 8
depression suffered by, 10, 11, 12, 27, 61
divorce of, 12–13
Coppola, Nicolas Kim. *See* Cage, Nicolas
Cotton Club, The (film), 27–30
critical reviews, 33, 35–36, 39, 41, 46, 48, 51–53, 57–58, 60–61, 64–66, 71, 72, 76
Crowe, Cameron, 21
Cruz, Penelope, 72
Cyclone (roller coaster), 60

Index

Darnton, Nina, 33
Deadfall (film), 52
depression, 11
divorces, 69, 75
Dreyfuss, Richard, 62

Ebert, Roger, 41, 48, 58, 64
Estevez, Emilio, 30
Evans, Robert, 29

Face/Off (film), 65–66
family, 6, 8–15
  divorce of parents, 12–13
  famous members of, 13–14, 16, 21
Family Man, The (film), 71
fans, 76–78
Fast Times at Ridgemont High (film), 20–21
fatherhood, 50
Feldman, Ilene, 26
Ferrari, 43
Figgis, Mike, 58
financial success, 43–44, 52
Finney, Albert, 58
Fire Birds (film), 47
Fulton, Christina, 46, 48, 50

Gere, Richard, 28–29, 30
Godfather films, 9, 13–16, 28, 32
Golden Boy (play), 20
Gone in Sixty Seconds (film), 71
Guarding Tess (film), 52

Honeymoon in Vegas (film), 50–52
Hopkins, Anthony, 61–62

It Could Happen to You (film), 53, 54
It Happened in Paradise (film), 53–54

Jewison, Norman, 40, 41–42

Kael, Pauline, 39

La Brea Tar Pits, 55
Leaving Las Vegas (film), 6, 56–58, 60–62
Lee Strasberg School of Acting, 17–18
Lemmon, Jack, 58
Lifetime Achievement Award, 62
Lowe, Rob, 30
Lynch, David, 48

Malkovich, John, 70
Maltin, Leonard, 24, 36
mandolin, 72
marriages, 58–59, 67, 69, 73–75
method acting, 17–18, 35
Milland, Ray, 58
Mitchell, Elvis, 76
Moonstruck (film), 40–42
Moore, Demi, 30
Moore, Dudley, 58
Mr. Blackwell's Worst Dressed List, 74

name changing, 21–23
Navajo language, 76

Oscar award, 56, 57, 61–62

Outsiders, The (film), 21

Pacino, Al, 15–16
Peggy Sue Got Married (film), 7, 34–36
Penn, Sean, 20–21, 27, 30, 61
Pennino, Albert (grandfather), 8
Pennino, Francesco (great grandfather), 8
personal life, 36, 44–46, 50, 54–55, 58–59, 73–75
Presley, Lisa Marie, 73–75

Racing with the Moon (film), 27
Raising Arizona (film), 36–39
Rat Pack, 30
Red Rock West (film), 52
Reiher, Peter, 39
reviews. *See* critical reviews
Ringwald, Molly, 30
Rock, The (film), 62–64
roller coasters, 60
Rowland, Mark, 36
Rumble Fish (film), 23–24

Saturn Films, 71
Scientology, 75
Shadow of the Vampire (film), 69–71
Shire, Talia (aunt), 6, 8
Shue, Elisabeth, 57, 58
Snake Eyes (film), 66
sports cars, 43
Strasberg, Anna, 35
Strasberg, Lee, 17–18, 35

tactile dome, 9
tattoos, 26
Travolta, John, 65–66
Troisi, Massimo, 62
Turner, Kathleen, 7, 34, 35

Valley Girl (film), 25–27
Vampire's Kiss (film), 46
Viores, Chris, 20

Wild at Heart (film), 48–49
Windtalkers (film), 75–76
Woo, John, 65–66, 75
Wright, Jenny, 36, 43

Picture Credits

Cover photo: © Getty Images North America
© Associated Press/AP, 20, 32, 45, 59, 60, 63, 74
© Bettmann/CORBIS, 16, 22, 75
Lauri Friedman, 77
© Pacha/CORBIS, 68
Photofest, 7, 14, 17, 18, 24, 26, 29, 31, 34, 37, 38, 41, 47, 49, 51, 53 (both), 54, 57, 64, 66, 70, 72
© Reuters NewMedia Inc./CORBIS, 43
© Roger Ressmeyer/CORBIS, 9

About the Authors

A former editor of children's books in New York City, Corinne J. Naden also served four years in the U.S. Navy as a journalist. She has written more than seventy books for children and lives in Tarrytown, New York.

A native New Yorker who lives in Brooklyn, Rose Blue has published some eighty fiction and nonfiction books for children. Two of her books were adapted for young people's specials aired by the NBC television network.